I0621721

Lessons on Seduction

E. Pettersen

www.blackvelvetseductions.com

ISBN 978-1-912768-87-5

Published 2020

Published by Black Velvet Seductions Publishing

Lessons on Seduction Copyright 2020 E. Pettersen
Cover design Copyright 2020 Jessica Greeley

All rights reserved. No part of this book may be used or reproduced in any manner whatsoever without written permission, except in the case of brief quotations embodied in critical articles or reviews.

This book is licensed for your personal enjoyment only. This ebook may not be re-sold or given away to other people. If you would like to share this book with another person, please purchase an additional copy for each recipient. If you're reading this book and did not purchase it, or it was not purchased for your use only, then please return to your favorite book retailer and purchase your own copy. Thank you for respecting the hard work of this author.

All characters in this book are completely fictional. They exist only in the imagination of the author. Any similarity to any actual person or persons, living or dead, is completely coincidental.

Acknowledgments

Thank you to my friends from the Wattpad writing community, especially Dasha Lamtsova, a talented writer who encouraged me to make the most of this story. I am grateful to my friends, Sherri and Caroline, and my family, particularly my mum, Ay Hwa, and my husband, Geir, who motivated me not to give up. And to you, dear readers, for taking the time to read Lessons on Seduction! It really is an honor.

Chapter One
Welcome to my Playground

Julian
First semester at Montville State University, August

"Baby, come back to bed," she purred, grabbing my arm.

"I need to get to class. There's no time to sleep in." I sat on the edge of the bed, gently loosened her grip, and kissed her forehead.

"Oh, honey, please, just one more time."

"There's a coffee machine on the kitchen bench. Help yourself to it on the way out."

"But—"

"You were good, sugar." I leaned forward and ran my hand along her smooth, tan, inner thighs. I slid my index and middle fingers inside her wet slit, pulled out, then licked them to taste her scent.

Melina Montes, or Mindy, was a college student in her prime.

Her flavor? Spicy and aromatic.

***

She was a sexy hellcat whose tits were popping out of her low-cut tank top when I recognized her across the room at a party last night. Dark hair: check. Dark eyes: check. Tiny waist and a fucking banging body: check, check.

She and I had had casual sex before, so it didn't take long for the familiar flirtation to turn into a make-out session, which resulted in business in the bedroom in my apartment, where she was a star.

Mindy was a little minx who knew how to satisfy a man. Her naked body was a piece of caramel cake, with small droplets of brown candy on the peaks of her breasts, and a smooth pussy that flowed cream so tasty and hot.

She fucked like a pro and knew how to handle my cock with her mouth. She started on the head, tasting it with her tongue, before using her suction technique, which was spot-on perfect.

Sixty-nine was my favorite number, so while she worked her magic on my cock with her lips, I snacked on her exquisite pussy. That pussy had a landing strip of short, dark hair, which I inhaled to take in her aroma. She was musky, sensual, and pleading to be licked.

My tongue landed on her landing strip, giving it gentle licks. Then my mouth dove into her core, nipping, sucking, and circling the ripe center with my wicked tongue. Her whimpers and mewling grew louder as I continued eating her while pinching her perfectly plump nipples with my fingers and thumbs to stimulate a little more pleasure. Those nipples were divine—they were territory that I'd visited from time to time before, nibbling, licking, and devouring them until they were sore.

"Oh my God, oh my God." Mindy's filthy mouth broke away from my cock and prayed to a divine deity.

I continued to roll her nipples between my fingers while feasting on her clit, wanting more of that pussy cream. Her body quivered as I continued with the motions, bringing her to a state of euphoria.

"Fuck, Julian, I'm going to come!" Mindy screamed.

I broke my kiss, positioned myself on top of her, and grabbed a condom. Once I had it on, I slid my hard, throbbing cock inside her, pounding into her sweet, wet pussy at a paced speed, until she screamed unfiltered pleasure peppered with obscenities. We both came hard and fast before I collapsed onto her body, catching up on my breathing. A minute later, we lay in silence, and Mindy's head rested on my chest. She played with the contours of my chest and stomach, tracing her fingers from my sternum to just above my love trail.

"Your abs. They're so fucking rock hard," she whispered, before falling asleep.

I'd just had the fuck of my life with Mindy. I'd known her for years, and she would come onto me like a cat in heat. We were amicable, but I wouldn't call her a friend, so it was a case of acquaintances with benefits. You see, I met her through my sister, Vera, years ago—they both went to high school together and studied law in college. We hooked up from time to time, but that's all it was.

After a night of little sleep, I woke up at seven, showered, and got ready for class. The mirror reflected a clear image of a man with mahogany hair and light bags under his dark, burnished eyes. I stared at the man, who was six feet tall with broad shoulders and a muscular build, thanks to my daily routine at Evolve Gym. The exercise initially helped me with a few back problems and eventually became a habit of taking care of myself. I lathered my square, unshaven jaw and started shaving for a fresh, clean look.

There's a faint scar, just above my right eyebrow, which serves as a reminder of my youth, when a little shit by the name of Wilson Cole shoved a swing bench into my forehead. It's a memento to remind me that the world is full of shitheads, and probably only twenty percent of the population are decent people worth having a conversation with.

I didn't mind the heavy nights of sex, but there was one problem—I had morning classes to teach and needed at least a double shot of coffee on the way to the archaeology department. Being a teacher's assistant/tutor while completing my PhD in archaeology at Montville State University meant I had to be alert and upbeat in front of the class. Based in the coastal city of Lester Harbor, in the state of Montville, the university had a leading archaeology research center.

As for Mindy, I didn't have time for anything more than a flirtationship. She managed to find her way out of my apartment later that day and left her black, lacy thong, which I threw in the bathroom bin. My name isn't Julian Carpenter Richland, the thong-collector. My middle name is my mother's maiden name, by the way.

I saw college girls like Mindy all the time. In class, at the gym, in the library, and in bed. She was no exception to the rule, and she wasn't the woman of my life, but she sure knew how to fuck.

I wasn't going to waste my time in meaningless, empty relationships, let alone listen to shallow conversations and empty giggles. Nah, it wasn't my style. Plus, I had an ongoing arrangement with Saira Quinn, a woman whose business was pleasure and pain.

Chapter Two
Goodbye, Cameron

Sapphire
Mid-September

"Cameron?"

An icy silence infiltrated the clean air in the sterile, sunlit room. The only thing that broke the peaceful ambiance was the sound of my voice.

"We go back a long way, you and me. I'll never forget when we first met in junior high. I was new in Lester Harbor, and you said I was the prettiest girl you had ever seen. Oh, we were just kids." I threw my head back and laughed at the bygone days.

"You were the lovable Cameron Oliver. We sat in church together and held hands during the sermons. Oh, my goodness, you had such a beautiful voice when you sang *Amazing Grace*. You were like an angel."

I sighed, toying with a strand of long, cocoa-brown hair that fell over my left shoulder.

"Then, when we started our first day of college together, you combed your hair, which really brought out your beautiful green eyes."

Those evergreen eyes were shut behind a veil of unconsciousness.

"For years, I've loved you, but our worlds are growing apart."

I've got this. Everything will be okay.

"Was it worth it when you cheated on me? I thought we would wait for each other. That our first time would be together when we married. Instead, you threw me away for a night with someone you barely knew."

I was so fucking stupid. Now in my last year of college, I realized that I'd wasted years loving someone who shitted on my life.

Live and learn, Saph. Live and learn.

I stared at the unconscious man on the hospital bed. The photo of us on his bedside table, placed there by his mother, showed a broad-shouldered and athletic guy who had everything going for him. He practically threw his life away a week ago, shortly after I found out he was fucking another girl. We fought about it, and then he left me so he could drown his sorrows at a boozy party.

That was the night he chose to drive home drunk afterward. He nearly killed himself by driving at a ridiculously high speed off a quiet highway at around two in the morning, veering off the road and crashing into a tree. *Fucking idiot.*

So here he was, battered, bruised, broken, and unconscious in a hospital bed. His right arm was in a cast, and so was his right leg. People said it was a miracle that he was still alive, and the medical staff believed he would slowly recover.

"Cameron, I wish it didn't have to be this way," I whispered.

He couldn't hear me, but I wasn't doing this for him. I was doing this for me. I had no idea when he would wake up from his coma, but I wasn't going to put my life on hold for him. It hurt to think of those bitter memories with Cam, so I had to cut my losses. It was now or never.

"Cameron, I cannot do this."

I removed the sapphire and gold ring he'd given me and placed it on his bedside.

"Are you okay?" a feminine voice asked, as I felt a soft hand gently clasp my shoulder.

I turned around to my new friend, Vera Richland. We'd met at a book club on campus early in the semester a few weeks back, and she became my rock of support amid the drama. She'd driven me to Saint Andrew's Hospital to visit Cameron that afternoon.

I felt a shiver run down my spine and rubbed my arms.

"Saph?"

"Right now, I'm not okay. However, I will eventually be fine. Just not right now," I confessed.

"I'm really sorry, Saph. I think you're doing the right thing, and I'm here for you."

Vera's comforting hug, which reminded me of soft velvet, engulfed my slender frame. A feeling of warmth began to flood my empty heart, and I felt a tsunami of relief.

"I've learned something, Vera," I said, slowly breaking away from the hug.

"What have you learned, sweetie?" Vera asked.

"The world sees Sapphire Blake as a conservative woman who is too afraid to dare. However, that's not who I am anymore. God, I was such a fucking people pleaser," I drawled, rolling my eyes.

"So, what are you going to do about it, hon?" Vera's dark eyes looked into mine.

"I'm not going to give a shit anymore." I smiled sweetly.

"That's what I kept saying from the moment we met," Vera responded, lightly touching my arm.

I turned away from Vera and moved one step closer to Cameron. I placed his limp hand in between my palms, caressing it gently.

"Cameron, I am saying goodbye to you. When you wake up, I won't be here. I'm doing something I should have done a long time ago. I am moving on."

Friday, a week later

"Toss or keep?" I asked Vera, holding up a pink cardigan with frills at the cuffs.

We were in the middle of updating my wardrobe, and it was in dire need of a makeover. Our mission was to free my closet of démodé outfits, which would be donated to a secondhand clothing store.

I enjoyed watching Vera's mouth twitch when she eyed the frills of the old cardigan.

"Definitely toss!" She laughed, picked up the garment, and threw it into a large, black plastic bag, which was filling up fast.

"How about this one?" I questioned, dangling an oversized, black turtleneck jumper.

"Honey, nobody would wear that, even if you paid them." Vera's bluntness was one of the reasons why we'd got along ever since we met. It was a blossoming friendship, and we bonded like a house on fire.

"What about the top I'm wearing?" I dared to ask.

"Lose it. It's fugly."

I pulled my top off, revealing an old, faded, light-blue bra.

"Get rid of that bra too," Vera commanded, as she made herself comfortable on my bed.

She was gorgeous, with caramel locks, dark eyes, and a toned body, reminding me of a hot fitness instructor I once saw on television. I was attracted to her forthrightness, her boldness, and her brilliant mind. She was in her final year of law school, and I believed she would make a terrific lawyer one day.

"Do it for me," she encouraged, tantalizing me with her raised eyebrow and coy smile.

"You first," I challenged.

"Alright, then."

Vera removed her tank top and bra, revealing a pair of bouncy breasts. Her nipples were perfectly round, dark, and looked deliciously edible. I sucked the air in and levitated into a state of heightened arousal. As I slowly removed my bra, I felt my nipples harden and tighten. My B-cup breasts were not large, but they were round and perky.

"Now, take off the rest." Vera's right finger directed me to remove my jeans and my panties.

"You too," I said with a lopsided smile, cocking my head slightly to one side. I took off my blue-rimmed glasses and placed them on my writing desk.

Vera removed her shorts and thong, revealing a neatly trimmed pussy, which elicited a shock wave of excitement.

"Come. Rest here with me." She patted a space by her side, and I obeyed her.

As I lay by her side, she stroked my hair and placed her luscious, full lips on mine. Her kisses were different from a man's kiss. They were soft, yet seductive. Playful, yet not forceful. She was stunning and intoxicating.

"Touch me," I begged her, as I started molding her breasts with my hands. It was the first time I'd played with another woman, and it was a naturally arousing experience.

We continued touching, kissing, and caressing each other for the next few minutes until Vera's phone buzzed.

"I have to take this call," she stated as she glanced at the screen.

"Sure," I coolly replied, leaning on my side.

"Mindy? What's up?" Vera slowly got up from the bed when she took the call.

I put my clothes back on, while watching a naked, nubile goddess pace back and forth in my room, with her cellphone to her ear.

"Whoa, slow down hon. Don't cry—it won't do you any good. I told you before, and I'll say it again. He's not the kind of guy you want to fall for. Trust me, I know him." Vera looked up at the ceiling as if she had heard this conversation before.

"If you can't handle it, then you shouldn't get involved with him." She pinched the bridge of her nose in frustration.

I began tidying my desk and put my glasses on while waiting for Vera's phone conversation to end.

"Don't. Don't do anything stupid. I'll be right over. Okay, bye." She ended the call, threw the phone on my bed, and picked up her clothes.

"What's going on?" I asked.

"It's a friend of mine. She's involved with my brother again, and now she's an emotional wreck."

"Sounds like a messy situation," I commented.

"Oh, you have no idea. I'll see you at the book club on Monday."

"What about this weekend?"

"Look, Saph. I hope you don't get the wrong idea, but I'm not after a relationship right now." Vera walked up to me and gently kissed my forehead.

"Don't worry, neither am I," I assured her.

"Good then. This doesn't change our friendship, right?" Vera asked, putting her clothes back on.

"Vera, we're good," I chuckled, flashing her a satisfied smile.

As I watched Vera walk out of my room, I thought about how my world was changing. It was time to open my mind as if it were a map to a world of undiscovered territory.

Chapter Three
Ménage à trois

Julian
Saira's apartment, October

I inhaled the scented candles that perfumed the air with an aroma of lotus and white tea. My eyes were cloaked in darkness behind the soft, silk blindfold. I rested on a royal-blue, luxury Baroque divan, patiently waiting for one of Saira's surprises. Aside from a studded leather collar around my neck, my body was naked and lathered in massage oil. My cock was hard and needy, throbbing for a wet, juicy pussy. I didn't want just any pussy—I craved for one that was personally handpicked by my mistress. Yeah, she was my Domme, and I served as her sub.

It wasn't the first time I had been inside Saira's stylish penthouse city apartment, which reflected opulence and style, thanks to her interior designer from New York. Saira was from old money, and she ran a family business with a tight fist, which, in turn, produced lucrative returns. She and I had a "business" relationship, which meant that I visited her on an "as-needs" basis, on her terms.

Saira came into my life a little short of two years ago when I worked for a catering company, serving drinks and canapés to guests at a wedding party she attended. I wasn't lucky enough to be born into wealth. Plus, my old man died of cancer when I was eight, leaving Mom a young widow with two little kids to raise. Regardless of the shitty cards life threw at us, my sister Vera and I got into college, intending to make our own successes. Still, I had bills and college fees to pay.

On the evening Saira and I met, the woman wowed me. She wore a tight, red, low-cut gown, revealing a pair of voluptuous breasts begging to be handled, and a high split that exposed her creamy thighs. The woman appeared at least a decade younger than her actual age—she was in her late thirties at the time, a ripe fruit that I desired to devour. Saira was a Norse goddess with her flaxen-blonde hair, light-gray eyes, long lashes, and red lips that I wanted wrapped around my dick.

Later that night, she made me an offer I couldn't refuse, to quote Marlon Brando in *The Godfather*. Long story short, I was in her office a week later, where I signed a contract, witnessed by her lawyer. The deal, in a nutshell, meant that I was hers for two years. In exchange, I would receive a considerable amount of payment transferred to my bank account in two installments—one for each contractual year, following the terms and conditions. The payment went toward my and Vera's college fees, private health insurance, a car, and daily living expenses. I also invested in an apartment of my own, moving out of the place I'd called home for years.

Vera knew about the arrangement; we were close, so there weren't many secrets we kept from each other.

Back to Saira—our deal was quite simple to understand. If she called or texted me outside of my teaching hours and college schedule, I was at her beck and call. It didn't matter if I was in the middle of a casual date or fucking some hottie. Saira came first. She and I enjoyed the sex, and she handpicked my playmates to fuck when we had a party of three or more at her place. She was a voyeur who enjoyed bondage, threesomes, foursomes, swinging, and whips. I fucking loved submitting to this woman.

We could screw anyone else we wanted, but there were a few rules:

1. Condoms.
2. Regular health checks.
3. Don't fall in love.

The last rule didn't bother me, as I wasn't the type who wanted to fall in love. Plus, I was a satisfied man.

***

I heard the fast click of Saira's heels on the marble floor, followed by slower-paced footsteps that accompanied her. The eagerly nervous tone of the feminine voice that spoke to Saira indicated that we had a fresh player who was new to our games.

"Julian, darling, I have a surprise for you." Saira's voice dripped with sweet relish.

"Introduce yourself to him, Emily." She coaxed my new partner for the evening.

"Hello," Emily purred, shoving her pussy to my face.

I breathed in her scent, then started kissing the core of her fruit, at first slowly, then picking up the pace with my tongue. I teased her with gentle sucks, while the sensations of sharp pain and pleasure struck my naked back.

"You like that, don't you, lover boy?" Saira harshly teased, while lashing my back with the cat o' nine tails.

Oh yeah, the cat—it was no surprise that she brought out the multi-tailed whip for a little foreplay.

"Mmm …" was all I could manage to say, while I fucked Emily's pussy with my mouth.

Emily's moans grew louder as my tongue jetted in and out of her core rapidly and repetitively.

"Suck on her harder! Harder!" Saira ordered, and I obeyed.

"That's it, lover boy. Suck on me harder," Emily encouraged.

Saira's flagellation stopped, then I heard her walk toward me. She got on her knees and started licking my shaved balls.

Oh, fuck, yeah! That's it.

I groaned into Emily's heated core, as Saira took the most sensitive parts of my body into her mouth, then released them, only to return with her lusty licks.

"Oh, that's it. Right there. Yeah. That's it, oh fuck!" Emily released a euphoric scream, as I continued devouring her.

I thirstily sucked Emily's warm juices when she came in my mouth. That was the feeling of bliss, right there.

A minute later, a pair of delicate fingers removed my blindfold and exposed my eyes to a pair of D-cup tits. I played with her nipples, which were light-pink and small, before taking each one into my mouth, giving each peak a gentle suck. I looked up and stared at a pair of wide-eyed green eyes, which gazed at me with desire.

"Do you like what you see?" Saira enquired, caressing Emily's oiled body.

"Mmm, I love what I see," I murmured, gently rubbing Emily's swollen clit.

Saira handed me a condom, which I placed on my stiff, thick cock.

"Here. Cuff him." She gave Emily a pair of steel handcuffs, and she dutifully obliged to the command.

Emily's bright auburn hair, which reminded me of autumn leaves in October, spilled over her shoulders.

"God, you're sexy, Emily. I want your pussy." I grinned, licking my lips.

Emily grabbed my shoulders, straddled herself on my body, and fit my cock into her tight, wet hole.

"Fuck him hard," Saira demanded, massaging and licking the redhead's generous breasts.

"Oh, you're so tight," I growled, as Emily pulled my hair back.

Our nocturnal activities continued until we were sated and satisfied. The scent of sex now coated the room, blended with the fading aroma of lotus and white tea.

***

The next morning, when Emily had left, I woke up with my cock in Saira's mouth. She paused, breathed me in, and continued sucking my dick.

"Good morning, love," I murmured, as she took my length to the back of her mouth, while her lips massaged my shaft.

Our morning play was sharply interrupted by the sound of the doorbell resonating throughout the apartment.

"Shit," Saira spat, when her mobile phone rang shortly after.

"Hello? Oh really? Alistair, you owe me one. Give me a sec, and I'll come out."

"Who's that, love?" I asked, turning on my side.

"It's my ex. He's leaving Damian with me a day earlier than we planned because he's flying to Dubai for an urgent business trip. They're waiting at the door."

Ten minutes later, after a quick shower, I sat in the kitchen, wearing a pair of jeans and a casual shirt, teaching Saira's ten-year-old son how to play Uno with a deck of brightly colored cards. I didn't mind kids. Would I have any of my own? Maybe one day, if there was someone I cared enough about. As for Saira, I had two months left of the contract, and then I was out of there.

I needed to move on.

Chapter Four
Just the way you are

Your nearness strikes into me like a red-hot operating needle.
Novelist and poet Malcolm Lowry to Jan Gabrial, January 6, 1934.

Sapphire
Vera's house, November

"What's his name, Vera?" I asked, as we walked up the stairs to her room.

Being in our last year of college, Vera saved costs by living at home with her mother, who was rarely in the house due to a hectic work schedule and a busy social life.

"My new boyfriend? His name is Ace. Ace Lockhart." Vera's cheeks blushed rose-red.

"So, when do I get to meet him?" I raised one eyebrow at Vera. I couldn't help but feel a tad jealous of the guy who'd won her heart.

"He'll be at Mindy's party next weekend," she replied.

"I don't think I'm welcome there. Mindy made it clear that she didn't hang out with church mice like me," I commented, rolling my eyes. People like her misjudged me because of my family's active involvement with the local church. I was more than ready to break free from conformity.

"She can be full of shit sometimes. She doesn't mind you, but she stands on the superficial side of the fence," Vera answered.

I looked around Vera's room and noticed a dirty towel on the floor, a half-eaten chocolate cake on her desk, and an unmade bed, covered with books and magazines.

"So, what's happening with Cameron, now that he's awake and recovering?" Vera raised her eyebrows, while her arms crossed and her right foot tapped the floor.

"He's undergoing physiotherapy to heal from his injuries, but it's going to take time," I responded.

"No, I mean, what's happening between you and him?"

I sighed and shook my head in exasperation. "He insists that he made the biggest mistake of his life, and he wants a second chance. He says it's the logical thing to rekindle our relationship, because our parents are so close, and we have a history together." I palmed my face and let out a stressful sigh in frustration.

"Please don't tell me you're falling into that fucking trap," Vera huffed.

"Would I eat my own vomit? I said we were done and that we could rebuild a friendship, but it stops there. There's not going to be a love story between him and me. Ever," I scoffed, shaking my head.

"High five!" Vera raised her palm, which I slapped in friendly jest.

"Cameron and every other guy on this planet are the least of my concerns right now. I'm more worried about upcoming exams," I commented, eyeing the photos on Vera's wall.

One framed sepia photo suddenly caught my eye—it featured a dangerously handsome man with dark hair and strong shoulders. The way he gazed into the camera lens was as if he wanted to tell a story with his mysterious, dark eyes.

"Vera, who is this? Is he your boyfriend?"

"Him? Oh, goodness, no! That's my older brother, Julian."

"He's a good-looking guy." I traced the outline of his muscled arm.

"Oh, honey, I'll give you one piece of advice: you don't want to get involved with him," Vera chuckled.

"Oh, don't worry, I won't. I'm freshly single, and I need some breathing space," I assured her.

"Breathing space … we all need that from time to time, hon. Don't forget to have a bit of fun." Vera revealed a Mona Lisa smile, pointing her index finger at me.

"Oh, I won't forget." I grinned at Vera.

"I'm going to have a quick shower. Make yourself at home. There's coffee and tea in the kitchen downstairs. You'll find it when you go past the living room," she said.

"Sure thing, sailor." I smiled at her.

I made my way down the stairs. I entered the modest living room, which featured a floral sofa with waxed oak legs, two beige recliners, a mahogany coffee table, and a white piano tucked in the left corner near the window. Speaking of the devil himself, my heart leaped in shock when I noticed Julian rummaging the bookcase, in a frantic search for a particular book.

"Oh goodness, I didn't realize you were in here!" I held my hand to my heart.

"Oh, hi." Julian turned around.

Our eyes were locked—there was no denying that there was an instant chemistry. You either had it, or you didn't, and there was no "lukewarm" with me. The man's frantic expression dropped, and his eyes softened when he saw me.

"I'm Sapphire, Vera's friend." I reached my hand out to shake his. He wiped his left hand on his jeans, then shook mine.

Oh, he's left-handed.

"I'm Julian." His espresso eyes expressed an element of honesty and gentle kindness, which I admired in a man.

"Hi, Julian." I smiled widely. I tilted my head to the side and tucked my hair behind my ear as a nervous habit.

"You've got the most interesting smile," he complimented.

"Julian … it's a beautiful name for a beautiful man." *Shit, did I really say that? Yeah, I did.*

At first, he didn't respond. However, he eventually let slip a small grin, then slowly fished a novel out of the bookshelf. "Here. It's one of my favorite books." Julian handed me a copy of *Quo Vadis* by Henryk Sienkiewicz. I took the book and stared at the cover.

"It's a good piece of fiction set in ancient Rome, based on events shortly after Christ's crucifixion. The author won the Nobel prize for literature in 1905," he explained.

"I love good books with a touch of history," I confessed.

"Then you'll enjoy reading that one." Julian pointed at the book.

"I'm a fan of the old classics, you know. One of my favorite books is *The Twelve Caesars* by Suetonius," I babbled.

I stared at Julian, who didn't react to my response. *Can someone take me to the back paddock and shoot me now?*

Then, slowly and surely, he broke the silence with a response.

"Suetonius's book is like an ancient version of *US Weekly*. However, if you like that kind of thing, you ought to read *Rome in Crisis* by Plutarch if you want to dig deeper into Nero and co.," he suggested.

"I work part-time at the main library at Montville State University, so I know where to find it," I admitted.

"Ah, I see."

"I'm studying for a Bachelor of Arts degree, majoring in political science and philosophy. I'm in my final year. What do you do, Julian Richland?" I wanted to know him.

"I'm working on my PhD in archaeology. I also tutor undergrads on the side, so I might see you on campus," he replied.

"I'd like that," I admitted.

Julian turned his back on me and scanned the bookshelf again.

"Ah! I found what I came for," he boasted, pulling out a copy of *The Art of War* by Sun Tzu. "It's a good book about strategy. It never gets old," he commented, turning toward me again.

"I know. I've read it." I smiled, staring directly at Julian's dark eyes. I then glanced at the white piano at the corner of the living room. "Who plays the piano?" I asked.

"I do."

"Oh, very nice."

"Here, come over." Julian gestured toward the long piano stool and encouraged me to sit by his side as he took a seat.

"Are you ready for this?" His grin melted my heart.

"Yes." I nodded.

He started playing Bruno Mars's *Just the Way You Are* so beautifully, and with impeccable pace.

I watched the way his hands moved as he struck each note and how intense his eyes were as they focused on reliving the memory of the song in his head. Being highly perceptive of people's personalities, I gathered that he was a quiet soul, an introvert with deep thoughts that were heavy in his head. I could imagine that he was often perceived as cold and arrogant, but I sensed that he had a kind heart. He wasn't particularly gregarious, but he showed his feelings with actions rather than empty words. I observed his hands as they tickled the black and white keys: they were large and his fingers were long. Oh, if they could only play me with the skill and finesse I was witnessing, I would be in heaven.

Julian's right shoulder and arm touched mine as they moved to make the melody resonate from the piano. My heart ached for my soul to be closer to this man, even though I sat by his side. I wanted that moment in time to slow to a halt, so I could continue to feel his presence.

I noticed that small parts of his short hair curled around the nape of his neck and behind his ears. His jeans, which perfectly wrapped his long legs, matched well with his light-blue Gant shirt, where his sleeves were rolled up to his elbows. His scent? Woody and dominant, with a heady mix of warm cinnamon and mint citrus. At that point, my lower abdomen melted into a flow of excitement and lust. A pool of wetness slowly filled my core as his presence ignited a spark in me.

When the song came to an end, Julian's shoulders relaxed, and his face was temporarily free from the stresses of the world.

"Did you like that?" he asked.

"You play so well. I'm impressed!" I touched his wrist, but he didn't flinch.

"I'll have to play a new song for you another time," he promised. "I'll see you around, Sapphire." He stood up and smiled, then made his way out of the house.

He remembered my name.

"Goodbye, Julian," I whispered. He was gone.

In all my life, I have never felt such an intensity of feelings that favored a stranger. After that brief encounter, I understood one thing: I wanted Julian Richland.

Chapter Five
Danger is sweet

Julian
December 1

I hated being late. I even believed that being on time was bordering on lateness. Yeah, I'm a stickler when it comes to tardiness—it's a habit I inherited from Frances, my mother, who ran a tight schedule with Vera and myself when we were growing up. This time, it was me who was behind schedule by seven bloody minutes, thanks to a student from my Roman History tutorial class who'd trapped me in the hallway, asking a myriad of pointless questions about the Second Punic War. I remarked that she was weeks behind, and she was going to fail if she didn't move on to Caligula. I was late for a Friday afternoon catch-up with Vera at *Calligraphy*, the university's book café, where the novels were classics, the ambiance was chilled, and the coffee was good.

Once I arrived at the café, I spotted Vera at a table by the window with Sapphire, the pretty blue-eyed girl who was at my mother's place a few weeks ago. *Sapphire.* Behind her glasses, her eyes were like the precious gemstone that was a derivative name of the Latin word for blue—*sapphirus.*

I walked over to Vera, took the chair beside her, and sat down, gazing at Sapphire.

"Hey, long time no see." Miss Blue Eyes initiated the conversation.

Vera introduced us. "Saph, this is my brother, Julian."

"Yeah, we already met." I threw a smug smile.

"He and I ran into each other in the living room at your place a few weeks ago. You were in the shower," Saph confirmed.

"Oh. As usual, I'm the last to find out." Vera cast a sardonic grin.

"Because it's all a big conspiracy, and the universe is out to get you," I poked Vera in jest.

"Jules, you're a jerk, but I love you," Vera laughed.

"What are you working on? Some project?" I leaned over and glanced at the laptop screen.

Ah, a dating site. The URL form read: www.matchmade.com/profile/sapphire-blake. The web page featured an advertising banner, and Sapphire's profile was right under it.

Name: Sapphire Blake.

Height: five feet and seven inches.

Hair: long, chestnut-brown.

Eyes: blue.

Likes: music, books, dancing in the rain on a hot summer day.

Personality: introvert, hard worker, open-minded.

Dislikes: gossip, Mondays, and exams.

Favorite quote: Live life, be free.

Star sign: Virgo.

"So, you're a Virgo. That means you're born in September, which is the month of your birthstone and namesake, Sapphire," I commented.

"No shit, Sherlock," Saph replied, grabbing a carrot stick from a snack bowl on the table.

Smartass. She had sass, which I admired in a woman.

"I'm helping Saph to create a profile on this dating website. She came out of a long-term relationship a few months ago, and it's time for her to try something new," Vera explained.

"I do not feel like doing this," Saph complained, releasing an exasperated groan.

"Get back on that horse again," Vera badgered, eliciting a laugh from Saph.

"Look, as much as I love you both, I need to get going now." Saph's blue eyes targeted mine as she started getting up from her seat.

"Stay, Saph. We don't have anything urgent to do, unless *you* have plans with someone new tonight," Vera answered.

God, Sapphire is beautiful. I wanted to kiss her rosy cheeks and lips.

"Stay. I insist," I assured her, gazing at her creamy, smooth, and slender neck. If I could just take one lick and nibble on it a bit.

"Okay, but I really do have to leave in five minutes. I can't be late for a family dinner tonight." Saph's shoulders relaxed, and she reclined against the back of her chair.

"Hey, let me take a look at this profile," I suggested, tilting the screen toward me.

"My brother's a pro at editing," Vera said.

Eyes: *Sapphire, like my name,* I edited.

Favorite quote: *Dulce periculum,* I added.

"What does that mean?" Saph asked, leaning forward. I noticed the top of her breasts pushed up. *Nice. Just lean forward a little more, sugar.*

"Danger is sweet. It's a Latin phrase," I replied, shifting my focus back to her perfectly symmetrical oval face.

"Oooh, exciting." Saph grinned.

We stared at each other briefly, before my sister cut into our unspoken conversation.

"So, how's it going with Jessie?" Vera interrupted.

"Is Jessie your girlfriend?" Saph's eyes widened with curiosity.

"She's someone I'm dating." There. No lies. Just the truth.

"They're secretly dating, because Jessie is a student in his tutorial class," Vera confided.

"My, you are a naughty boy," Saph teased.

"Exams are next week, and I'll be handing her assessment to a close colleague to ensure fairness with the results. After that, it's the end of the semester, and she won't be my student any longer." I relaxed.

"Mmm, you're trying to behave. How cute," the minx giggled, flashing her sapphire eyes at me.

"Cute is for teddy bears. Call me sexy or ruggedly handsome." I grinned.

"Okay, then. You're sexy and ruggedly handsome, Julian." Saph's voice bubbled with mirth.

"Hello? Guys, I'm still here," Vera reminded us. She sure knew how to cramp my style.

"Well, I *really* have to go now, because I don't want to be late for dinner." Saph stood up, smiled at me, and packed her laptop in her bag.

"It was good to see you again, Saph. Catch you later." I waved as she kissed Vera's forehead, then walked out of the café.

"Care to tell me what's going on?" Vera's fiery face fired at me.

"I swear to God, I never touched her!" I protested.

"Okay." She shifted her seating position and smirked while crowning her head to watch Saph walk toward the bus stop outside.

Wait a minute …

"You and her. Fuuuck." I ran my fingers through my hair and shook my head.

"Relax, Jules. We just kissed and played a little. That's all. She needed some fun after dumping her fucktard ex." Vera grabbed a cherry tomato and sucked on it.

"How's Ace?" I asked, changing the topic.

"He's okay," Vera answered.

"Vera, I swear to God, that guy's a fucking psycho," I warned.

I immediately knew Ace was a prick when my sister introduced us at a bar downtown two weeks ago. When Vera went to grab some drinks, the shit started feeling up some chick in a flimsy, barely-there dress.

Bad move, Ace. Bad move.

I told the fucker that if he hurt my sister, I would make his life a living hell.

Vera preferred an exclusive relationship and needed someone who could respect that. Unlike her, I was an "open relationship" kind of guy, and I was always upfront about it from the start with the people I dated and fucked.

My contract with Saira was coming to an end next week, and I had been casually seeing Jessie Caruso for the past few weeks. Jessie was an eager student, in more ways than one, from the start of the semester months ago. At first, I told her to back off, but she was insistent and demanded my exclusive attention after class. It was hard to resist her, especially when she revealed her D-cup breasts and fully waxed pussy. My cock submitted to her demands.

She could have easily passed for a *Playboy* centerfold, with her dirty-blonde hair and bewitching turquoise eyes. We had a few hot late-night sessions in an empty college classroom, where we fucked on the desk, on the floor, against the wall, and on one of the seats. Naturally, we were at a point where we'd decided to take it from casual sex to casual dating. Who knows what could happen?

As for Saph, I barely knew the girl and was keen to get to know her. She came across as an open-minded woman who didn't judge others. I didn't want just to get to know her body. I wanted to get to know her mind, her heart, and her soul.

Let's take it one day at a time.

Chapter Six
Hot Shower

Julian
Friday, a week before Christmas

"I don't want to let you go, love," I whispered, burrowing my head into Saira's slender neck, as my cock jetted in and out of her.

She was on all fours on my bed in my apartment, begging me to keep going, harder and faster. A pair of leather handcuffs shackled my wrists, but I could still massage her buttocks as I continued grinding into her.

"Oh, please, Julian, don't fucking stop!" she cried out.

After a while, I could no longer restrain myself as I felt the pressure building and growing stronger. I finally pulled out of her and ejaculated streams of cum on her lower back. Saira was on the contraceptive coil, and we were both clean, so we were cool with going bareback.

"Where's Jessie? Why couldn't she join us this time?" Saira asked a moment later, after she uncuffed my wrists.

"She's out with some friends. Besides"—I pulled Saira closer into me—"I wanted to spend this afternoon alone with you."

I kissed Saira's lips and pulled back, staring into her gray eyes. "I'm going to miss you like hell, love," I murmured.

"You know," she began, "I can offer you something that doesn't require a contract. I'm a woman of my word when it comes to payments."

"Pray, do tell," I spoke, in between kisses.

"I propose that we continue our rendezvous on an 'as needed' basis. I call you, and you choose to play or not to play. Fair?"

"Sounds fair."

"When you choose to play, I will choose to pay. Same account, no time span, and the choice is yours. Understand?"

I nodded my head. I wasn't ready to let go of Saira completely. She was my heroin, and it would take time to taper off the drug.

"I have to leave. I'm meeting the new candidate for the position you've left available." She smiled coquettishly.

A few minutes later, Saira had left and I was heading toward the shower.

Sapphire
Later that Friday evening

"Are you sure it's fine for me to stay over?" I asked Vera, who decoded the keyless lock and let us inside Julian's spotless two-bedroom apartment.

Vera and I were heading out to town that evening to meet Mindy and a few others at Rory's Sports Bar. First, we needed to dump our bags and get ready at Julian's high-rise home, set smack bang in the fusion of the bustling city.

"Yeah, my brother doesn't mind if we crash at his place every once in a while, like tonight," Vera answered.

"Cool." I eyed the sterile, open-plan kitchen as we walked past it. I gathered that this guy must be a neat freak—he and his sister were opposites in that respect.

"Besides, he would rather have me safe at his apartment after a night out in town than in some strange cab back to the burbs at three in the morning," Vera assured.

"I don't have a big brother, so I wouldn't know what it's like to have someone looking out for me the way Julian does for you," I stated.

"Jules can be a little overprotective, but he's gotten better over the years. Just dump your stuff in the guest room. I'm going to the convenience store downstairs to get some snacks. I'll be back," Vera said.

"Ok, make sure you get something gluten-free for me," I hollered, as Vera left the apartment. When I was eight years old, I was diagnosed with celiac disease, a severe allergy to wheat. Therefore, I could only eat gluten-free meals.

I walked around the spacious living room and was amazed by the floor-to-ceiling windows that showcased panoramic city and river views. It defined downtown luxury living, with its high ceilings, white leather sofas, high-end Italian appliances, and sleek, polished wooden floors.

I wondered how he could afford all that—I would have to ask him for some real estate tips when I move from home.

I turned left, headed toward the direction of bedrooms, and stopped when I reached the main en suite bedroom. This must be Julian's room. Curiosity may have killed the cat, but it wouldn't get the better of me, so I dared.

I dropped my bag on the floor and walked into the master suite, which featured two dimly lit lamps and a king-size bed with a charcoal duvet and matching pillows. The unmade bed was the only untidy element in this otherwise clean home, indicative of either his most recent sexual activity or his forgetfulness to make the bed up. I doubted that it was the latter. As I walked past the bed, I noticed leather handcuffs on the crumpled duvet. The soothing sound of water running in the shower caught my attention, enticing me to take a sneak peek in the bathroom.

The bathroom door was left open at a forty-five-degree angle, and the pull of temptation gravitated me toward it. I was curious. I usually did not pry into the privacy of others, but I had never seen a naked man in real life, and I was ready to find out.

Oh, my lord! There he was in the shower, a beautiful man in all his splendor and glory. Julian was wet and naked, reminding me of the marble statue of the biblical, nude David by Michelangelo. Droplets of water ran down his hard, taut, body, all the way to the curve of his muscular back and firm buttocks, then along his sturdy legs. He rinsed the soap off his broad shoulders, chest and slim waist. His body tapered down like a perfect V, and delicate veins ran along his muscular forearms. His penis was thick and admirable, even in its relaxed state, and his testicles hung below. Eyes closed, he lifted his head to absorb the streaming water, and ran his long fingers through his hair, washing out the remaining shampoo foam, which flowed downward.

The heavenly sight of Julian in his nakedness, together with the fresh scent of the citrus body wash, triggered my nipples to harden and the inner walls of my vagina to clench, eliciting a wetness that coated my labia.

Julian's eyes opened and fluttered rapidly, making direct contact with mine. "OH, FUCK!"

"Oh shit, I'm so sorry! I was looking for a spare toothbrush and didn't realize you were here!" I babbled in a flustered state. I was a bad liar.

He turned off the shower faucet, grabbed a towel, and started to dry himself slowly.

"Did you enjoy the show, *Sapphire*?" Julian smiled smugly, emphasizing my name when he spoke.

"I, uh, I'm staying over with Vera tonight, as we're heading out for a girls' night. I hope that's okay with y-you," I stammered.

"Oh, it's more than okay with me, love. However, you haven't answered my question." Julian's mischievous eyes dangerously twinkled with devilish delight.

"I like what I see," I admitted, gazing at the towel, which he now wrapped neatly around his firm torso.

"Good. Now, come here, baby. Touch me."

I took one step closer to Julian and stroked the blade of his left shoulder with my right hand. My fingers traveled down his chest and stomach, drawing him to release a groan of pleasure.

"That's it. Lower."

"Lower?" I gasped.

"Yes. Further down south, if you get my drift."

My fingers traveled below his navel and down to where the towel met his skin.

"Stop."

"Stop?" I raised my eyebrows.

"Yes, stop," he commanded.

Julian's hands swiftly reached around my neck and untied my halterneck top, exposing my bare breasts to him.

"You're exquisite." His long, dark lashes lowered as he gazed at my topless body.

I sucked in the citrus-flavored air as he began rubbing my nipples in circular motions with his rough thumbs.

"I want to see all of you. I want my cock in your pussy," he coaxed.

"Julian," I moaned.

He pinched each nipple in delight as if he'd found a pair of shiny, new toys to play with. He continued this movement repetitively and harder, causing me to gasp in pleasure and pain.

"Ouch!" I yelped, triggering him to stop immediately.

"We can try a bit of gentle foreplay," he suggested.

"Not now. Vera's going to be back soon," I blurted, pulling my top up and tying the strings back behind my neck.

"Wait. Don't forget this." Julian opened a drawer under the sink and handed me a new toothbrush, unopened in its plastic packaging.

As I reached out to grab it, Julian's hand gently caressed mine.

"Next time, *Sapphire*, you can join me in the shower," Julian murmured. "Would you like that, love?" My seducer whispered into my ear before removing his hand from mine.

"I would love that," I flirted unashamedly.

It felt so natural to be responsive to this man.

"I'd love to teach you a thing or two." The academic's playful eyes held me captive before I started backing out of the bathroom.

As a whirlpool of arousing sensations rushed throughout my body, I darted out of the bedroom and picked up my bag, just in the nick of time, because Vera strode into the living room with a bag of snacks.

"Is Julian home yet?" Vera asked.

"Uh, yeah. I think he's in the shower," I replied calmly.

"Oh, good. You know, you can leave your bag in the guest room. You don't have to lug it around the entire apartment."

"Oh, sure."

"Saph, don't let my brother seduce you," Vera warned.

***

Hours later, when Vera and I returned to the apartment after a night with the girls, Julian's bedroom door was shut.

I heard the sound of a woman moaning with pleasure, coupled with loud grunts that belonged to Julian.

"That's his girlfriend, Jessie. She must've missed him this evening." Vera grabbed my hand and pulled me to the guest room.

An arousing chill ran down my spine. I remembered Julian's words earlier that evening. *I'd love to teach you a thing or two.* I realized that I was spiraling into an abyss of seduction that was too deep to crawl out of. It was too late for heaven to help me.

Chapter Seven
Auld Lang Syne

Sapphire
December 31, New Year's Eve

It's okay, Saph. You've got this.

Breathe. One. Two. Three.

I leaned over the faucet and stared at my reflection in the public bathroom mirror. I was at the Sky Bar rooftop nightclub at the top of the Hilton Hotel downtown. Vera had invited me to hang out at the club and celebrate New Year's Eve with her, Ace, Mindy, and some friends. Of course, Julian was there when I'd arrived earlier that evening. He was enjoying the open atmosphere with a glass of gin and tonic in one hand, while Jessie whispered sweet nothings into his ear.

"You got this," I told myself, fighting off Wicked Anxiety in the bathroom.

Keep telling yourself that, Saph. You're a twenty-two-year-old virgin who can't get a man to fuck you—Cameron wouldn't even bed you after years of being together, Wicked Anxiety taunted.

Shut up, anxiety. You're a bitch.

Look into the mirror, Saph. What do you see? Lady Hope stepped in, whispering in my ear.

I saw a slender woman with straight, chestnut hair, who'd swapped her glasses for contact lenses.

What else do you see? Lady Hope led on, pushing Wicked Anxiety away.

I saw an emerging beauty in a lustrous, blue satin, backless cocktail dress, featuring a plunging halterneck.

A modelesque woman with dark curls brushed past me and smiled as she headed out the door, back into the club. The depths of my heart warmed up, and I knew that I was ready to walk out in confidence.

"Saph! Come over here! Let's get a photo together," Vera shouted, waving at me as I walked toward her and the gang.

"So, is the church rat staying in the hotel with us?" Ace laughed, taking a swig of his beer.

"Yeah, my room is right next to yours and Vera's, so you'd better tone it down, because this church rat don't take your shit," I replied, stabbing him with a piercing stare.

I didn't like Ace very much—he reminded me of a young Val Kilmer from *Top Gun*, but he was an obnoxious guy. Tonight, he was especially bad-mannered, but Vera dismissed his behavior, blaming it on the alcohol.

I glanced at Julian and his girlfriend, who was all over him like a rash. He looked divine and sophisticated in his suit, white shirt, Burberry cufflinks, and black tie. Julian was a deliciously dominant alpha among the men in the club that night, and my heart felt a tug of pained yearning. His eyes caught hold of mine, staring at me for a moment before they flickered away like sparks fizzling in the dark. It was as if I didn't matter to him. With Jessie there, I was a complete stranger. The she-devil glared at me, before placing her seductive hands on Julian's jaw, bringing him to her lips.

While they kissed, Jessie's cold eyes glowered at me. Her message was clear: *he's mine.*

"Everything alright?" Vera tapped my arm.

"I left my lipstick on the bathroom counter," I recalled, before walking back to the public restroom.

Luckily enough, my Guerlain rouge lipstick was still on the counter, so I picked it up and tucked it in my handbag. As I was about to open the door, it swung at me, and a pair of hands shoved me against the wall.

"As you know, Julian and I have an open relationship. I normally don't mind Julian's flings, but *you!*" Jessie shouted, before slowly releasing me. She pointed her index finger at me. "You're a dangerous cunt. I don't trust him around you because he can't take his eyes off you!"

My blood boiled with anger, like bubbling broth about to overflow. "You know what? You're right," I replied, narrowing my eyes at her. "I am dangerous, Jessie, and you better watch out. If all it takes is one glance between Julian and me for him to forget you, then he was never yours to begin with." There. I said it. The words weren't pleasant, but I didn't take shit from anyone who pushed me around. With that, I pushed past Jessie and walked out of the bathroom.

A few hours later, as we chanted the countdown toward midnight, holding sparklers in one hand and champagne in the other, I noticed a cute blond fellow in a dark shirt and a few of his friends cheering close by us. I overheard a drunken version of *Auld Lang Syne* belted out by a group of partygoers in the background, interrupting the countdown. At the stroke of midnight, as we sang out "Happy New Year," I grabbed blondie by the collar of his shirt and kissed his soft lips. After breaking the kiss with the blond mystery man, I gazed at Julian, who pulled away from Jessie and raised one eyebrow at me.

"Way to go, Saph, and Happy New Year!" Vera hugged me, interrupting the hidden exchange between her brother and me.

She wore a slinky gold sequin number and shone brighter than the fireworks in the sky.

***

A little while after the festivity of the New Year's Eve celebration, I headed toward the bar to get a Porn Star Martini. I noticed Mindy at the corner of the club, drinking alone.

"Mindy? Is everything okay?" I asked her.

She glanced up at me, wearing a look of desperation.

"I tried—" Her eyes watered with tears.

"I tried to make him fall in love with me. I gave him everything, and he's broken my heart." Her voice was frail.

"Mindy, maybe you gave him too much too soon. Guard your heart," I advised.

"I know, but these feelings. It still hurts," she protested.

"Did he ever tell you that what you had was a relationship? Were you dating, or was it just the sex you were both after?" I asked.

"It was just sex. He never led me on. It's just that I expect more than what he wanted to give," she replied, before proceeding to tell me her story. "I've known Julian for years, because Vera and I were in the same class in high school. When he was a senior, we were in grade nine, and he used to walk Vera and me home from school, making sure we were safe."

"That's so sweet," I commented.

"That's Julian. He was quiet, an introvert, and he excelled in his academic work. He was in the student council, and he played some football, but he was never one to brag. Of all the girls he could have taken to prom, who do you think he took? The captain of the cheerleading squad?"

"I don't know, Mindy. He doesn't seem like the kind of guy who relishes in his own vanity," I responded.

"No, he took Kelly Jane Miles, a girl who had cerebral palsy. He decorated the wheels of her chair with small snowflake lights, and he gave her the most beautiful corsage of roses. That's the kind of guy he is," Mindy stated.

She paused and wiped away a stray tear, then continued to tell me more about Julian.

"He once picked me up from the mall when my parents were out of town. A bunch of girls, who were supposed to be my ride, ditched me and I was left stranded at ten o'clock with no money for transportation. I called him and he drove from the other side of town just to pick me up and take me home."

Mindy took a sip of her vodka and lemonade, sucking what was left in the glass through her straw.

"Things changed when I started college. I had just moved out of home and he helped me move my furniture into the apartment. I offered to make dinner, then we started kissing, and he made love to me for the first time. Saph, Julian is an incredible lover. Honestly, he's one of the few guys I know who can give me an amazing orgasm. Whenever we were intimate, he truly made me feel alive," Mindy admitted.

"After years of casual sex, I thought that there was a chance for a real relationship to happen. I always thought he would be the one. That, one day, he'd commit to me. However, he recently told me that it would never happen and that he was done with our hookups."

"Mindy, is he commitment-shy?" I queried.

"Vera said that ever since their dad died, he's been hiding his feelings behind a wall. He transformed from being such a happy kid to one who was emotionally withdrawn. The Julian we know today keeps to himself. He's a sexually open guy, but he hides his feelings well," Mindy explained. "I thought I could change that." Her tears now spilled on the table, and she was frantically wiping them away from her face.

"Honey, you can't change him. He has to want to do that himself. Besides, we have to accept that this is who he is, and you can't make him fall in love with you. When he falls in love, he will choose that for himself. But you can't wait for him, because it may never happen," I stressed.

"But I want him so much! I want him to fall in love with me! I've never lost anything to anyone," she cried.

"Mindy, stop. Please, you're hurting yourself. One day, there will be someone you will meet in your life, and you will understand why it didn't work out with Julian or anyone else. And this guy, whoever he may be, will be a helluva lucky guy," I assured her, patting her arm.

"Really?"

"Really."

I took a Kleenex from my clutch and passed it to Mindy, who dabbed her tear-rimmed eyes. It was clear to me that she lacked the emotional strength to get into a relationship with Julian. She was used to getting what she wanted and handled rejection poorly. Julian had never lied to her. Sometimes, people's expectations were higher than what we could offer, even if we were upfront from the start. This was where I felt that I understood Julian.

"I'm going to the hotel room now. I'm tired and it's time to get some beauty sleep." I got up from the stool, glancing at the elevators.

"I'll join you for the elevator ride. I need to sleep too." Mindy crumpled the Kleenex in her hand.

Just then, I received a text message from Cameron.

>Happy New Year, Saph! I still love you. Can I please see you?

Chapter Eight
To Hell and Back

Sapphire
January 1, 1:00 a.m.

"Go away, Cameron," I muttered, before returning his text message with a simple reply.

>Happy New Year, Cam! Wish you all the best.

He responded with another text.

>Can I come to you? I miss your beautiful face.

Booty call. Nope, I was not going there.

>I'm kinda with someone tonight. See you at church on Sunday.

>Okay then. See you on Sunday.

Like the prodigal son, Cameron had returned to church life after his accident. His folks and mine were close friends, so it was inevitable that I would see him from time to time. I meant it when I wished Cam the best. He and I once had something special, but that was over. We'd rekindled a friendship, but he wasn't particularly important to me anymore.

"C'mon, let's take the elevator down," Mindy prompted, reminding me that we needed to get some sleep.

"Sure, let's go," I replied.

Our heels clicked on the marble tiles toward the elevators. We had just missed the last lift, which Julian and Jessie had taken. I caught a glimpse of them as the doors closed and couldn't help but feel a twinge of envy.

A few exhausted partygoers were waiting for the lift with us, including one barefoot, inebriated woman who boisterously complained that the fairies had stolen her shoes.

"Is there a mirror in your panties, babe? I think I see myself in them." Some boozy slimeball suddenly grabbed me from behind.

In response, I instinctively swirled to face the perpetrator and stomped on his foot hard with my stiletto heel.

"Oww, you frigging bitch! You're so ugly no one would touch you anyway!" Slimeball yelped in pain, hobbling away.

"Are you alright?" Mindy asked me, frowning with concern.

"Yeah, I'm fine. You know, the princes of this party turned into pumpkins after midnight." I rolled my eyes at the pitiful sight of drunkenness.

Just as the elevator doors opened again, I noticed Vera storm out of the club, with Ace following her, shouting obscene profanities.

"Mindy, you go ahead. I'm going to help Vera," I instructed.

"Sure. Make sure Vera's going to be okay." Mindy stepped in the elevator, eyeing the quarreling couple before the doors closed.

"I was right there! I saw you feeling her bum!" Vera cried, turning at Ace in defiance as he tried to grab her arm.

"What about you, you hypocrite? You've been quite the filthy Jezebel, flirting with half the club tonight," he sneered, attempting to grasp her arm again.

"Flirting with half the club? I was there by your side the entire time! Stop deflecting! I saw you feeling that girl's ass," Vera protested.

"You snide, little bitch! Don't you talk like that to me in front of these people!" Ace snarled, seizing her wrist.

"Let go! You're hurting me!" Vera screamed at Ace, who twisted her arm with an inflamed aggression.

"LET HER GO, ACE!" I stepped in, not giving a fuck that a new batch of people who'd arrived at the foyer to wait for the elevator were staring at us.

"If you touch her like that one more time, I swear I'm going to call the cops, or worse—Julian," I shouted, pulling Vera's arm from Ace's tight grip.

Ace stepped away from Vera and stalked toward me, ready to unleash a negative attack with his raging hostility. The russet-haired brute towered over me, balling his fists in an attempt to appear dominant and intimidating. I smelled a concoction of ale, wine, and stale cigarettes on his foul breath.

"YOU fucking stay out of it and mind your own bloody business, church rat!" Ace spat in my face.

I held my position and did not cower from the abusive bully. I refused to remove my eyes from his perforating glare. Deep inside, I was terrified that he would hit me, but I refused to cower from the oppressor. I did not show my fear. He took one step back, then masked his aggression with a charismatic smile, while straightening his collar. He was the devil in disguise beneath the mask of handsomeness.

"Shit, Vera, I'm sorry, darling." He shook his head with bitter remorse. "I've had too much to drink. Let's go to bed." He spoke calmly, gently stroking Vera's head and kissing her golden caramel hair.

"I've got this." Vera tapped my arm, and together, she and Ace took the next elevator down. I joined them and a crowd of retired party goers who'd left the club to go home.

When we arrived at our floor, I walked in pained silence behind Vera and Ace until we reached our hotel rooms.

"Goodnight, babe! Happy New Year!" Vera hugged my body and kissed my cheek, as Ace opened the door to their room.

After sliding the keycard into the slot near the knob, I opened the door to my room and was only too glad to be surrounded by the serene quietness. I changed out of my clothes, washed the makeup off my face, and removed my jewelry before slinking into a pair of comfortable pajama pants and a gray t-shirt.

"Happy New Year," I muttered aloud, crashing into the soft double bed.

2:00 a.m.

THUD!
THUD, THUD!
Holy shit, what the heck was that?
I woke up in a state of shock, hearing a trail of screaming abuse drilling through the wall, coming from Vera and Ace's room.

"You were eye-fucking that guy tonight! Don't lie to me, you fucking cunt!" Ace screamed.

"You're blind, Ace! You did all the eye-fucking and feeling up another woman tonight, you bastard!" Vera defended herself.

I realized that the nightmare was real when I heard another bang and Vera's scream coming from the other side of the wall.

"You fucking bastard!" I heard Vera cry.

"You know what? You deserve this, you little whore!"

"STOP IT! PLEASE! I beg you, stop!" Vera's defenseless voice screamed.

Thank God the walls in the hotel room were thin, because I now knew exactly what was going on and what to do. Vera needed help! I took my keycard, dashed to the hallway, and knocked on the door to Vera and Ace's room.

Knock, knock.

I tried again and heard muffled voices before the door slowly opened.

"Vera, come!" I pushed past the door where Ace stood and gently pulled her to me, hugging her tightly.

Vera was a complete mess. Blood oozed down her lower right lip, which was swelling rapidly. Her hair was disheveled, and a red mark was imprinted on her right cheek below her eye. The bruises wouldn't show up until the following day. I had never seen a woman so strong become so broken and vulnerable in a matter of minutes. The bastard had hit her.

"You did this! How could you?" I blurted.

"Mind your own bloody business, church rat! This is between Vera and me," Ace threatened.

"You deserve to burn in hell!" I retorted, quickly moving toward the door, taking Vera with me.

We raced back to my hotel room, and I quickly used the keycard and slammed the door shut to ensure the monster wouldn't come after her.

THUD, THUD, THUD! Ace banged the door several times and yelled out a series of menacing threats, before retreating to his room. Then everything went quiet.

The rapid beating of my heart and Vera's soft sobs were the only sounds that followed, infiltrating the room with fear and sadness. Vera, who was shell-shocked, cried in my arms as we sat on my bed. I rocked her gently, attempting to calm her down.

"Everything will be alright. He's gone now. He's gone." I hugged her and cried with her as she wept a flow of tears. Our tears became one, as we grieved and lamented over the damage that the psychopathic monster had created.

"Where's your phone?" Vera slowly pulled away as her eyes searched wildly around the room.

"Here." I reached for my mobile phone on the side table next to my bed, unlocked the screen, and handed it to her.

She then called a number and handed the phone back to me, commanding one word: "Julian."

I placed the phone to my ear and heard his voice.

"Hello?"

"Hi, it's Sapphire. Vera needs you—it's an emergency. Can you come and see her now?"

"Is she hurt?"

"Yes."

"Where is she?"

"She's in my room. 817."

"I'm on one floor above. I'll come straight away."

**

The next few minutes felt like an eternity.

Ace was at it again, banging my door, then begging Vera to come back to him, claiming that it was all a mistake.

"Ace is a mistake," Vera whispered, as I cleaned her face with a wet tissue.

"It's not your fault, honey. He's a psychopath, and they're smart at hiding their flaws," I said.

The hallway was quiet again after Ace gave up and returned to his room. Only then did I notice, when Vera pushed her hair away from her face, that her right ear was bleeding.

"Shit, what did he do to your ear?" I gasped in shock.

"He bit me." Her eyes widened in fear. No doubt she was reliving the sequence of events.

I rushed to the bathroom to grab a hand towel and dampened it with water. I was furious at the motherfucker for hurting my girl and hoped that Julian would teach him a lesson or two.

"Here, let me clean the sore." I gently wiped her bloodstained ear with the cloth and checked that the bite didn't warrant stitches. Thankfully, the wound appeared shallow.

There was a light knock on the door.

"Vera? Sapphire? It's me," Julian's voice resonated from the other side.

I quickly got up from the bed and opened the door, letting him in. He looked over my shoulder, moved past me, and hugged Vera tightly, soothing her, while she nestled her head into his chest, breaking down in sobs of tormented pain.

"Who did this to you?" Julian asked.

Vera's espresso eyes stared at her brother with a silent plea for help. "Ace?"

Vera nodded in response.

"I'll fucking kill him," Julian growled. "Where is he?"

"In the room next door, to the left," I answered.

"Get a cold bottle of Coca Cola out of the mini-fridge to numb the pain on Vera's lips and give her some water to drink," he suggested.

"Of course," I replied, taking Vera's hand.

Julian's eyes flashed a hot blend of distress and vengeful hate before he let go of Vera and stepped out into the hallway.

In the next few minutes, we heard Julian's voice raised at Ace, followed by a heavy bang against the wall. I only hoped that Julian was not hurt.

"NEVER hit a woman, you fucking piece of shit!" Julian roared.

"If you ever lay a hand on my sister or any woman again, I'll hunt you down and make you wish you were never born!"

A moment later, Julian knocked and I opened the door. He stepped inside and glanced at Vera, who was wincing in pain as she took a few small sips of cold water. His left fist was swelling fast, and his knuckles were bright red, as he held Vera's half-opened travel case and handbag in his right hand.

"Pack your stuff. We're going now." Julian threw the travel case, strewn with clothes hanging out of it.

Vera hobbled to the bed and grabbed her handbag, opening it to check that her mobile phone was tucked inside. She carelessly rolled the clothes that had fallen out of the travel case and stuffed them back inside.

"I'll take you to the medical center to make sure you get checked first thing in the morning," Julian vowed, stroking his sister's forehead.

"What about Jessie?" I asked.

"What about Jessie? She's not your concern," he retorted. His eyes flashed a signal of dark annoyance.

As Vera slowly lifted her travel case, Julian stepped toward me.

"Thank you for looking out for my sister tonight." His eyes softened and expressed gratitude.

"Don't thank me. Nobody deserves abuse," I replied.

"Saph, I won't forget what you've done for my family."

He then looked over to Vera, who walked toward him. His eyes were clouded with heartache.

"Thanks, Saph. I owe you one." Vera smiled weakly.

It was evident that it hurt for her to smile with her busted lip. The lip would heal, but the emotional scars would never be forgotten.

"You don't owe me anything, Vera," I reassured her.

Vera nodded, and Julian took her in his arms, walking her out of the room. Before he left, he turned and gazed at me. He nodded his head, then gently closed the door. We had an unspoken and implicit understanding. In Julian, I had a friend.

After that night, I learned that Julian had broken Ace's nose and knocked out a tooth. It's incredible how news travels fast.

Chapter Nine
Girls Just Wanna Have Fun

Sapphire
Friday, September 3, nine months later

Time had flown by and it did a lot of good for most of us, especially for Vera, who regained her emotional and mental strength from coaching sessions with a professional counselor. She, Mindy, and I received our college degrees from Montville State University, while Julian was awarded his PhD in archaeology. Professor Julian Richland now taught full-time at the university, focusing his research on a landscape archaeology project. Mindy and Vera worked for different city-based law firms and kicked ass in their careers. Vera was determined to use her profession to fight for victims of abuse, harassment, and wrongful discrimination.

Unlike Vera, Mindy, and Julian, I struggled looking for full-time work. I applied for both private sector and government jobs, with no luck. So here I was, still working part-time at the library, disappointed that my boss couldn't give me more hours, due to staff budget cuts. To make ends meet, I'd found a second job, working eight hours a week at an animal rescue shelter not too far from the city. My total earnings weren't great, but I made enough to leave home and share a downtown apartment with Vera.

Vera and I bonded well as roommates, and I especially enjoyed listening to her play on her sleek, black digital piano near the balcony in the late afternoons.

"I thought it was just Julian who played the piano," I commented one Friday afternoon.

"You never asked." Vera glanced at me, with her mysterious smile, then continued playing Beethoven's *Moonlight Sonata.*

"Julian's taking us out for dinner tonight," Vera said.

"Oh?"

"Yeah, it's his treat."

I saw Julian from time to time, but it was usually when he dropped off or picked up something from Vera at our place. He didn't come over very often, and why would he? He had his own life, and I had mine. Plus, he frequently traveled for conferences, his fieldwork project, and collaborative events with other universities. I still had Julian's book *Quo Vadis*, but the last time I tried to give it back, he told me, "Keep it for as long as you need it."

***

Dinner with Vera, Julian, and Jessie that evening was a somewhat mixed affair, starting with all sorts of pleasantries and ending in disconcerting awkwardness.

"How are your therapy sessions these days, Vera?" Jessie asked, grabbing a celery stick from her plate.

"It's going great," Vera quipped. "In fact, I see my therapist only once a month now."

"A healer named Hippocrates once said healing was a matter of time and a matter of opportunity," Julian told Vera, referring to her healing process.

"Oh, Julian, don't be such a bore, darling." Jessie feigned a yawn and patted his shoulder.

Her large breasts practically spilled out of her deep-plunge crimson dress, revealing a slip of the nipple when she leaned forward. A part of this turned me on, and I understood Julian's attraction to her, but another part of me cringed, considering we were at a restaurant where parents brought their kids. She then started toying with Julian's tie, and twirled the ends of his curling hair, before smothering him with face-sucking kisses that were inappropriate for Morgan's Family Steakhouse Restaurant.

I glanced at Vera, who shook her head at Julian. He took the hint and lightly pushed Jessie away.

"You just called Julian boring?" I scoffed loudly.

"The *professor* can be rather boring when he starts quoting Hippocampus and the rest." His former student's feline eyes sliced mine.

Vera snickered and Julian cleared his throat, but I couldn't hold back.

"It's Hippocrates, not hippocampus," I corrected Jessie, who hit back with a haughty laugh. "There's a big difference between a Greek physician and a brain part, Jessie," I continued, carving a sliver of steak and taking a bite.

The rest of the dinner was uncomfortable and ended with Julian and Jessie leaving early, skipping the best part—dessert.

"Honestly, I don't understand them," Vera said, as she dived into her creamy, delicious crème brûlée.

"It's simple. She's incredibly sexy, and she's probably a queen in the bedroom. He's not complaining either," I replied, tasting the sweetness of my gluten-free chocolate panna cotta.

"Damn, I should have gotten some tips from Jessie," Vera exclaimed.

"You don't need tips from her. You already are sexy," I said, while I gazed at Vera's gorgeous face and scanned her fit body.

We walked along the riverside boardwalk later that night, and Vera's arm linked with mine. I breathed in the scent of jasmine flowers and plucked one from a nearby shrub. The night air was temperate and mild, and a cool breeze gently blew past us.

"This is from me to you." I placed the jasmine flower behind Vera's ear and stroked her hair.

She then planted her soft, silky lips on mine, eliciting a low moan from my mouth.

"Vera," I breathed as my heart raced rapidly.

"Saph." Vera slowly withdrew from me. Her eyelashes lowered before she looked up with the spark of a thousand lanterns amid the dark, cloudless sky.

"I know how you feel about Julian," she murmured, touching my lips.

"Vera, I—"

"You don't need to say anything. He wants you too."

And there she was, with her Mona Lisa smile, which mystified me.

That night, we slept in Vera's bed, naked and unashamed. She touched and kissed me, and I returned her kisses with an intoxicated fervor. I touched the silky skin of her perky breasts and kissed them softly, taking the dark, hardened nipples between my lips. My tongue teased and swirled around each nipple before I began to suck hard. When she stroked my mound, I gasped, wanting her to explore more of me. However, she stopped there.

"You don't belong to me, Saph. You belong to Julian," she whispered, stroking my hair.

I lay in her arms, staring at the darkness in her room before closing my eyes and drifting in a deep sleep.

Tuesday, September 7

I loathed blind dates. Especially when your date doesn't show up after thirty minutes.

His name? Tristan Reid, a twenty-six-year-old IT consultant and a dog lover who, like me, enjoyed the rain on a hot summer day. Except, I never got to meet him in person because he didn't show up.

>Hey Tristan, were we supposed to meet today?

I hit the send button and waited for a few more minutes. No response.

The waitress, Rosie, took my order, aka dinner for one, at *Calligraphy* book café, then a familiar man walked inside, slinging the strap of a leather Cambridge satchel over his shoulder. He was easily recognizable by his swagger and the way he dressed—he wore a simple, dark-blue button-down shirt and corduroy pants. His deep espresso eyes communicated a combination of familiarity and relief when he saw me.

"No glasses?" Julian stood over me, dropping his satchel by my side.

"No, I wear contact lenses these days."

"So, how've you been, Saph?"

"To be honest, I just got stood up by a date."

"Oh? I pity the man or woman who stood you up." He grinned and sat by my side.

"Why, Julian?"

"Because I'm your date now." Julian's smile widened as he cocked his head at an angle, capturing my eyes with his demanding gaze.

"How's Jessie?" I asked, breaking the spell.

"Aah, Jessie. Is that all you think of when you see me? Jessie?"

"Excuse me, sir, would you like something to eat or drink tonight?" Rosie asked as she came to our table.

"Uh, yeah. I'll have what she's having and a cappuccino," Julian replied.

He watched Rosie take the order before she returned to the counter. She was attractive, no doubt, and he noticed it too.

"No, Jessie is not all I think of when I see you, Julian," I answered, then paused. "It's just that she doesn't like you and me hanging out, and I don't want to be messing with her man," I added.

"Jessie is insecure around you. I don't blame her." Julian chuckled, then moved in closer to me, not allowing any additional space between us. I felt the warmth of his solid arm, which gently rubbed against mine.

I breathed in his heady, citrus scent, which sparked an immediate arousal to my body, infiltrating my soul.

"I'm not hers to keep," he said.

"You've been with her for nearly twelve months, Julian. You live together. You must be serious about her," I pointed out.

"Not really." He smirked and shook his head, stealing a glance at my hands on the table. He then placed his hands next to mine so that our fingers touched. "She and I ... We sleep with other people. We fuck other people, and we fuck each other sometimes."

"Sometimes?" I raised my left eyebrow.

"Here you go, sir, madam." Rosie bounced at our table with our coffees and sugar-sprinkled, gluten-free jam doughnuts.

"Dinner?" Julian laughed.

"Yeah, dinner," I chuckled, taking a bite of my doughnut.

"Jessie moved out of my apartment two months ago. We split up as a couple, but we still have sex on occasions."

"Well, your life sounds more interesting than mine. I can't even get a blind date to show up!" I frowned, evoking laughter from Julian.

"Well, how about we make a deal?"

"I don't like deals. They're usually too good to be true."

"You'll like this kind of deal, love."

"Go right ahead and make your offer."

"I finish my last lecture at five-thirty on Tuesdays, so how about I rock up here at six every Tuesday and reserve this table for us?"

"Do you mean, like a coffee date?"

"Yeah, or we can even do dinner if you're hungry," Julian laughed, glancing at the jam doughnut.

"Here. Take a bite. It's good." I took his doughnut, enticing his mouth with it.

Julian took the bait, biting softly into the sweet dough. I gently brushed the sugar off his lips with my thumb. He took my sugared thumb, then kissed and sucked on it tenderly. "Mmmm, heavenly." He closed his eyes and sighed when I withdrew it.

I fluttered my eyes shut, inhaled the aromatic air around us, then looked up again. "I'll do it," I declared. "Six o'clock at *Calligraphy* every Tuesday."

He took my hand, then brought it to his lips, kissing it smoothly, while his dark angel eyes pierced mine.

Chapter Ten
Birthday Treat

Sapphire
Tuesday, September 14

"I thought to myself, 'Who is Sapphire Blake?' and the truth is, I really don't know you," Julian mused.

Sitting by my side, he leaned into me and murmured, "Sapphire Blake, I would like to get to know you."

It was our second date at *Calligraphy*, and true to his word, Julian was sitting at the same place at six o'clock on the dot. He had ordered two coffees and gluten-free jam doughnuts, which were neatly presented on the table.

"Tell me about yourself," he said.

"Sure thing, Sigmund."

"Don't worry, love. I'm no Freud, so your mind is safe with me."

"Smooth, Sigmund. Really smooth." I grinned.

"Well, where do I start? My parents are David and Sylvia Blake, and they are both engineers for an energy company. They live in a four-bedroom home fifteen minutes north of the city, and my younger brother, Roland, is in the eleventh grade."

"Go on." Julian lifted his hand and stroked his chin with his thumb and forefinger as if he was in deep thought.

"Stop with the Freudian act," I flirted, nudging his leg with mine.

He chuckled, nudging my leg back into place. Except he didn't retract his leg—it moved into my space, and his thigh touched mine. I slid my hand under the table and gently touched him. His hand reached for mine and tenderly played with my fingers, exploring and feeling their warmth. I felt the firm smoothness of each long digit, reminding me of his expert piano playing.

"I don't play a musical instrument, but I used to sing in the choir at my local church," I continued my story.

"Which church?"

"Northern Lakes Baptist Church," I replied.

"Aah, I see. So you believe in God."

"I do," I replied. "But there's a difference between religion and spirituality. I've met a lot of religious people who aren't necessarily nice, kind, or loving. With me, I will admit that I am flawed. I don't love all people, and I won't apologize for that either," I continued.

"Nor should you." He sipped his coffee.

"I can't read into the future, so I tend to overanalyze people and situations. I'm notorious for being late, and I eat junk food instead of salad." I laughed softly, tucking a stray hair behind my ear.

"Sapphire, you are an exquisitely flawed and beautiful soul. Your flaws make you perfectly who you are. Alluring. Ethereal. Recherché. A treasure," Julian said.

"And what of beauty? I've seen your choice of women, and they are beautiful. You have admirable taste, and it appears that you have a gratifying lifestyle," I complimented.

"I like to think of myself as an Epicurean rather than a Stoic. I am a person devoted to a lifestyle of sensual enjoyment, especially when it is mixed with fine food and wine," Julian declared.

"Well then, I am glad we met. For too long, I have lived the life of a Stoic, accepting the status quo without complaining," I sighed, smiling at my date. I took a bite of my doughnut, which oozed with strawberry filling, then sipped the rich taste of my cappuccino to quench my thirst for the aromatic warmth.

"Saph, I want to let you know that I'm not obsessed with appearances. After all, we are like the leaves that begin dewy-fresh in the youth of spring, become golden in the prime of summer, and brittle in the autumn, eventually fading away into nothingness."

Julian paused, then looked at me.

"It's the mind that showcases a world of beauty, and the heart that keeps it warm." He gently tapped my forehead as a gesture of appreciation of the mind. His eyes crinkled as he grinned, revealing a wide, pearly-white smile. He didn't smile very often, but how wonderful it was when he did.

"I see the warmth of your heart in your smile," I commented.

"How does that make you feel, love?"

"It's delightful. I feel like I'm walking on air."

Just then, a local band started playing on the small stage, disrupting our flow of thoughts.

"Do you want to get out of here?" I asked, ignoring the remainder of my sugared doughnut.

"Yes." Julian's eyes pooled with clouds of lust and curiosity, quickly peeking into my loose, low-cut, little black dress.

I had wanted to feel sensual that evening and to feel free from the confines of restrictive garments, so I was completely naked beneath the dress.

"Where do you want to go?" I looked at Julian.

"How about we go for a stroll along Harlow Gardens?" he suggested, opening the café door so we could leave.

"I'd like that, Julian." I smiled, slightly tilting my head.

"C'mon, then. We don't have all day." Julian grinned, showing his pristine teeth again. He extended his left hand for me to hold, which I duly took.

***

Only a twenty-minute car ride away from the city, Harlow Gardens was home to magnificent ornamental ponds, lush-green lawns surrounded by coniferous trees, and an open-air gazebo. Julian and I walked along the empty lovers' pathway, hand in hand, toward the green forest, before coming to a halt.

"What do you believe in, Julian? Do you believe in a god, or goddess, or the universe, or nothing?" I enquired. I was curious to know the man better.

He frowned, then looked away, before changing the topic.

"See that gazebo over there?" He pointed with one hand while placing the other on the curve of my lower back.

"Yes, I see it. Shall we go there?" I gently pulled him toward that direction.

"I was six years old when I fell from climbing that gazebo. My dad sat me down and told me that we all fall at some point in our lives. When I see it now, I remember him," Julian reminisced.

"He was right," I said. "We all fall at some point, Julian. We just get back up again and keep falling and getting up."

A moment later, we both sat in the gazebo, gazing at the empty field. There was something so peaceful and serene about nature in the darkness.

"Julian, when did you learn to play the piano?"

"Ah, yes. I was twelve when my mother took us to a music store. Vera wanted to see a piano, and I was just bored. There was an old pianola in the corner, which I was curious about." Julian's eyes shone with happy mischief. "I tore the sheet off, and long story short, we walked out of the store with another piano and Mom signed us both up for piano lessons," he concluded, placing his arm around my shoulder.

"You must have been quite a child," I giggled, as his hand caressed my shoulder.

"What else would the mysterious Sapphire Blake like to reveal about herself?" Julian offered a half-smile while his eyes peeked into the gap between the cloth and my breast.

"Well, it's my birthday today," I confessed.

"REALLY?" Julian's eyebrows shot up in surprise.

"Yeah, I don't make a big deal about birthdays. Each day is a gift," I answered.

"Indeed. So, love, what can I give you for your birthday?" He took my fingers toward his sensual mouth, kissing them gently.

I thought of Julian's mouth tasting every inch of my body, from the nape of my neck to the back of my knees, then down to sucking my toes. Most of all, I wanted him to taste my sex; I wanted his lips and tongue right there, at that very place that was virgin territory, untouched by man. I also craved to know what it was like to touch a man's cock—not just any man's cock, but Julian's cock. A pool of sweet, sticky wetness surged between my thighs, and my nipples hardened.

"Julian, I've never been pleasured by or given pleasure to a man before. I want you to show me what you know. I want you to teach me." I placed his hand underneath my dress and between my legs.

"Then, I think we're done talking this evening," he murmured. He lowered his head on mine and brushed his lips on my mouth, before pulling my body close to his and taking the kiss further with his wicked, expert tongue.

Julian

"I want you to teach me." My virgin sweetheart guided my hand to her mons.

The moment she uttered those words, I wanted to educate her about sex—I am, after all, a teacher. I wanted to personally teach Sapphire Blake, the birthday girl who had just offered herself to me, about a new world. She would soon experience a renaissance. An enlightenment. Nirvana.

"Julian? Will you start tonight?" Sapphire asked, as my hand explored her round, naked buttocks.

She had no panties on. Incredible. My fingers played with her unshaven mound, feeling her maiden hairs, before finding their way to her wet, creamy vaginal lips. God, I wanted to fuck her senselessly; I wanted to give her my dick, to deflower each of her holes in every perverse way, and to fill her with my seed.

Fuuuck, my cock hardened, ready to take her in. All I had to do was touch her to make her quiver and beg for me, then the prize—her virginity—would be mine. However, she was more than just a quick fuck. I planned to create a sexual union between us, where pleasure would turn into bliss and energize into something so deep and powerful. She was, in every way, a treasure.

"J'ai envie de toi," I murmured in her ear as I massaged her virgin mound.

"Julian? What does that mean?"

"I want you."

I continued kissing her supple lips, as my hands removed her flimsy dress over her head, unveiling the seductive nakedness of a love nymph. I gazed at Sapphire's swollen, round breasts, which advertised puffed, hardened nipples surrounded by large, light-pink areolas. What treasure! This was my discovery, and I was a lucky man.

"Oh, Julian, please!" the vixen wailed, as my mouth descended on each of her nipples, greedily taking them in with generous sucks.

"Please what, pussycat? Please stop?" I paused, looking into her dark, dilated eyes.

"No! Please don't stop! I want to feel him. I want to touch him too."

"Patience, love. You'll have him," I promised, whipping out my erect penis, guiding her hand to wrap itself around it.

"Feel that. Feel what you've done to me, Saph." I coached her to play up and down my shaft.

"It's so magnificent and proud." Her thumb curiously played with the head, causing my cock to twitch.

"All your work," I responded, as she rhythmically massaged my shaft, eliciting a deposit of pre-ejaculate.

"Is it mine?" she asked, staring at my dick.

"Yes. It's yours, but for now, I want to try something you'll enjoy."

I moved away for a second, then got down on my knees, spreading Sapphire's legs wide so that I could get a full view of her fruit.

"What are you doing, Julian?"

"I'm giving you a birthday treat you'll never forget," I replied, burying my head in between her legs. I spread the folds of her sex with my fingers and kissed her.

"Ah, gorgeous," I murmured, breathing in her *cassolette*—her sweet, natural perfume. I ran my tongue on her flushed, swollen vulva, licking and sucking the clitoris as I greeted it.

"Oh, Julian! Ooh! Don't stop!" she moaned over and over again, while I continued fondling her with my mouth.

My tongue probed into and out of her vagina several times and danced with her clitoris, then repeatedly and rhythmically flicked the wet, slippery skin until she orgasmed.

"OH MY, JULIAN! I'm coming!" she screamed, as her vaginal juices rushed into my mouth.

"My sweet Sapphire," I murmured into her heavenly cunt, before kissing it goodnight.

When the calm came after the storm dissipated, she slowly put her dress on, and I moved up to sit by her side, caressing and stroking her back.

"How did I taste?" Saph asked.

"You tasted deliciously sweet." I kissed her earlobe, then her jawline, and finally, her plump lips.

We continued our passionate embrace until she broke away from my mouth for some air.

"Julian, your cock. I never got to …" Her low voice drifted.

"Don't worry, darling. This is just our first lesson. Let me take you home." I tucked my shirt in my pants, before zipping up.

"I just don't, I mean—"

"Don't fret, love. There will be plenty more lessons to come."

Sapphire Blake was ripe and ready for tantric sex, and I had the pleasure of educating her.

Chapter Eleven
Erotic Massage: A Sexual Experience

Sapphire
Calligraphy, Tuesday, September 28

"Sorry I couldn't make it last week, love. I had to attend a work conference upstate."

Julian kissed my forehead as he stooped down and sat next to me at our usual place.

"You're here now." I held his hand.

He sported dark circles under his eyes, most likely due to lack of sleep. Yet he appeared deliciously wicked with his unshaven jaw and unkempt hair.

"Did you miss me?" He ran his finger along my arm. The touch alone sent a shiver down my spine.

"Was I supposed to miss you?" I teased.

"I was hoping so. Absence makes the heart grow fonder."

"I thought it was absence makes the heart go yonder."

"I believe the original saying was absence makes the heart grow fonder, unless it makes the heart go yonder."

"In other words, out of sight, out of mind?" I raised one eyebrow.

"Not with you, my love." Julian's thumb gently rubbed my hands in a circular motion.

My love. He called me his love. His dark eyes stared at mine while he clasped my hands. Yet, his face was riddled with stress.

"I'm not a good man, Saph."

"Julian, you are honest. That makes you a better man than a man who falsely advertises himself as *a good guy*," I pointed out.

He stared intensely at me, oblivious to the noise of coffee grinding at *Calligraphy* that evening. "Honesty still doesn't make me a good man, darling." His eyebrows knitted, creating two vertical lines between the brows.

"But you are a good man, Julian! I know you are! Underneath your layers, there is a good soul who deserves so much more than what this world has to offer."

"Saph, I'm going to be upfront with you. I won't promise you marriage, kids, and a house with a white picket fence. I'm not that guy."

I felt an invisible, hard smack on my chest, which tightened with anxiety.

He doesn't care about you. Wicked Anxiety stepped in, sensually wrapping one arm around Julian's chest, stroking it with carnal leisure.

Step aside, bitch! Lady Hope bumped Wicked Anxiety's hip, setting her off balance and pushing her aside.

Lady Hope firmly placed both hands on Julian's shoulders. *Look at him, Saph. He's yours for the taking, but he's weaning off old habits.*

Old habits die hard, or never at all. Wicked Anxiety viciously glared at Lady Hope.

Have faith, Saph, and trust your instinct. You've got this under your control. Lady Hope coyly smiled at Wicked Anxiety, who eventually vanished.

Lady Hope winked at me before she dissipated into thin air.

You've got this, Saph.

"Julian, I don't care how many women you've fucked or are fucking. I've got an open mind, as long as you're playing it safe."

"I'm playing it safe."

Julian paused, then shook his head. "You truly deserve better than what I can offer, Saph."

"Oh. Is that it? Is it so easy for you to give up on what we started? Well then, I'm already disappointed," I replied. I quickly masked my crestfallen face with a sophistical smile and withdrew my hands from the table. Just as I stood up to leave, I felt a tight grip on my wrist.

"I don't give up so easily, Saph. Don't leave without me," Julian urged. His eyes burned with furious fervor, scorching my soul as desire licked my inner thighs. "If you're willing to accept openness, then you are a saint."

"I've always had a soft spot for sinners, and I fucking want you, Julian."

Twenty minutes later

"Come in, love. Don't be shy," Julian coaxed, as I stepped inside his apartment. "You know your way to my bedroom." He lightly spanked my bottom.

I placed my bag on the floor and entered the familiar territory. His territory. This time, his bed was pristine perfect, *sans* handcuffs.

"Come here, love." Julian unbuttoned my cream blouse, removing it altogether.

"What do you want me to do, Julian?" I asked.

"I want you to take everything off, then hop in the shower. I'll join you in a second. I just need to make a phone call."

I removed my clothing and folded it neatly on a modern, ergonomic swivel chair by the window. I turned to Julian, who was on the phone with a work colleague. His eyes widened, and his mouth formed a perfect O when he saw my body. I smiled, winked, and sauntered into the bathroom to have a shower. Not even a minute later, I felt a pair of warm hands massage my breasts as I stood under the heavenly, light waterfall that washed my body clean.

"Feel this," he whispered, pressing his penis against my lower back.

"I feel it," I responded breathlessly, moaning when he pushed harder against me.

He kissed my neck with hungry delight and manipulated my breasts to stimulate my senses. I squirted the citrus body wash from the dispenser, turned around, and started lathering Julian's body. His solid, muscled physique was a masterpiece—he had shaved his chest and pubic area, including his testicles. Dark hair feathered his arms and legs, accentuating his masculinity.

He returned the favor of body cleansing by massaging liquid soap along the curve of my hips down to my smooth, bare pussy.

"You're different." He explored my vaginal area, massaging the clit.

"Vera took me to a Brazilian wax clinic on Saturday," I revealed.

I'd be lying if I said it didn't hurt when the wax specialist removed all my pubic hair, but it was worth the pain to feel a smoother experience of heightened pleasure with Julian.

"Tell me, darling, is there something I should know about you and my sister?"

"Well, we've kissed, and she's seen me naked," I confessed.

Julian twitched his mouth, trying not to smile.

"Okay, it's a little more than that," I admitted. "She and I fondled each other a few times, but that's it."

"Hmm. I may have a chat with Vera afterward. The last thing I need is competition in the family."

"Vera wasn't kidding when she told me you were a competitive man!" I grinned.

A few minutes later, after a steamy shower of deep kisses and heavy petting, Julian gave me a white bathrobe. He dried himself with a towel, then walked naked into the bedroom.

"Come, love." He guided me into an impressively neat walk-in wardrobe the size of a small room. His clothes were meticulously presented on the left side of the room, while the shelves on the right displayed an assortment of sex toys and massage oils.

"Frankincense is known for its aphrodisiac properties. It relaxes, rejuvenates, and enlivens emotions," Julian said, handing a small vial to me.

I opened the cap and inhaled the spicy, woody aroma.

"Ylang-ylang is an exotic Asian scent that is used as a love potion. It effectively stimulates the senses." He handed me another bottle, which I opened and sniffed.

"Mmm, these are irresistibly intoxicating," I murmured, closing my eyes.

I felt Julian's warm hand caressing my cheeks, intensifying the connection between us.

"Will you make love to me tonight, Julian? Will my first time hurt a lot?" I asked, opening my eyes.

"Oh, Saph," Julian chuckled, then removed my bathrobe, letting it fall on the ground. "As much as I want to fuck you with my cock, lovemaking is a process. It's not just intercourse."

I felt so clueless, yet grateful for Julian. Cameron would never have given me this kind of experience.

"The Tantric philosophy of oneness and wholeness is about fully attuning our senses to our pleasure. It's not just a physical delight but a deeper experience," Julian explained.

He placed the frankincense vial, a hand towel, and a bowl of rose petals on a small tray, which he took to his bed. He then spread a large towel on the bed and guided me to it.

"The idea is that by involving your whole being in a sexual union without guilt, pleasure turns to bliss and brings radiance. Lie down on your stomach, sweetheart."

He lit two candles, perfuming the dimmed room with a blended fragrance of Indian rose and sweet almond oil. He turned on soft music, further stimulating my senses.

"In Tantra, a woman's satisfaction and orgasm are very important. These things, my dear, are what you're going to learn before we start fucking."

Julian applied the oil on my lower back, massaging from there toward my shoulders. He pushed his hands in one sensual movement, following my natural contours.

"Your skin is like silk," Julian complimented, continuing the sensual massage.

He moved both hands outward across each of my shoulders, then slid down to the rest of my back with his fingers. He repeated this movement several times over the next few minutes, increasing the pressure with a kneading rhythm.

He used the heels of his hands to caress my back and leaned forward, kissing the back of my neck, where the hairline met the skin. I felt the warmth of his body on top of mine, and his relaxed cock brushed along my back. He massaged the rest of my body, from my buttocks to my legs, then from my shoulders to my fingertips. The oil felt divinely warm on my skin, and I was fully aroused as Julian continued working on my body.

"Turn over, love," he instructed.

I turned to lie on my back and stared at Julian, who gently dropped a scattering of rose petals on my exposed breasts, belly, and genitalia. He bent over to press his lips on mine, gently sucking my lower lip and slipping his tongue inside my mouth. He increased the pressure of thrusting his tongue, encouraging me to mimic his movement before he eased off and moved downward, kissing my nipples, navel, and clitoris.

"Spread your legs wide, darling," he coached. I obeyed his instructions, revealing myself to him.

"That's it. Perfect." He massaged my swollen clit, which was wet with want.

"I'm going to taste you now." Julian's head lowered, and his tongue began weaving its wicked magic on my clit, lapping it with hungry desire.

I felt the familiar heightened sensation toward an orgasm grow stronger as his tongue sucked my swollen and engorged clitoris.

It's coming.

It's coming.

Then ...

"JULIAN!" I screamed in frantic ecstasy.

My hand pushed his head deeper into my pussy, which dripped with sweet juices from the orgasm.

After a moment of heavy breathing, Julian lay on his back beside me. "Would you like to return the favor?" he asked.

I nodded, sat up, and wrapped my fingers around his dick, which grew larger and stiffer as it sprang to life.

"It likes you very much," Julian teased, exposing a playful smile.

His cock twitched when my thumb played with its smooth head, rubbing the sensitive skin and touching the slit. I inhaled his heady scent, which aroused me.

"Gentle, love. Use some of the oil and start massaging along the shaft."

Julian took the oil and poured a few drops into my cupped palms. I then rubbed the oil with my hands and clasped his uncircumcised cock with my right hand. His hand guided mine to move up and down the shaft, caressing and pulling it with applied pressure.

"That's it, love. Oh, keep going," he encouraged, breathing heavier and faster.

He took my left hand, inviting it to gently play with his smooth, soft testicles while my right hand massaged his dick. My movements became faster and firmer, working in rhythmic motion, as Julian's breathing became thicker.

"That's it! Speed up, love!"

"NOW! FUCK, oh yeah! Fuck!" Julian's body tensed, then his cock ejaculated ribbons of cum, shooting at my naked breasts.

My right hand was covered with his warm sperm.

"Come here, darling," he urged, pulling my head down toward his.

He kissed me, then sighed before letting go.

"Next time, I'll teach you how to kiss a cock."

Chapter Twelve
Yuletide Pleasure for Two

A few days ago you were a goddess—and that was very handy, very beautiful, very inviolable. Now you are a woman.
Poet and essayist Charles Baudelaire to Apollonie Sabatier, August 31, 1857

Sapphire
December 24

"Julian, I'm a little nervous." I smoothed my deep-red, silk dress, which revealed slits on both sides of my thighs and an ample cleavage.

I wore a pair of red Jimmy Choo pumps to match the dress, and my hair was loosely swept back in an elegant bun, exposing the nakedness of my neck.

"Don't be, darling. You're beautiful, delicious, and fuckable," Julian whispered into my ear.

God help me, I silently prayed.

Julian had taken me as his companion to the prestigious Christmas Eve concert dinner at Customs House by the river. The dining room was opulent with Corinthian columns and cabaret-style tables that were clothed with flower arrangements. The walls were adorned with gold-laced mirrors, and the crystal chandeliers hung like heavy fruit from the ceiling. Lester Harbor's wealthiest and most prominent faces filled the room with an abundance of buzz and chatter. Dressed in their tuxedos, the men exuded both influence and affluence, while the women were spectacularly lush, extravagant, and beautiful.

I held onto Julian's arm as we walked around the room, looking for our assigned table. Tonight, he looked divine with his slicked hair, shaven face, polished shoes, and black tuxedo. I inhaled his scent of blended citrus and bergamot as he escorted me to our seats.

"Julian, thank you for taking me to the concert tonight." I glanced at my partner and smiled.

"Darling, I wouldn't dream of going with anyone else," he replied. "You've bewitched me."

Julian had taken special care before the evening to ensure that my three-course meal was strictly gluten-free, instructing the event organizer that I was allergic to wheat. When the musicians began to play, I slipped my hand under the table and clasped his hand.

"This is one of my favorite pieces. It's 'Concerto in G Major TWV 40:201' by Georg Philipp Telemann," Julian whispered.

"Julian, do you have a photographic memory?"

"I remember the things I'm passionate about, particularly music. It's a world of its own where I can escape to sometimes."

"I'm impressed."

"Vera and I may not have had much money growing up, but it didn't mean we were uncultured and dimwitted."

"You and Vera are incredibly bright."

"You can thank my mother for that. She was incredibly strict, raising us alone."

We ate our meals in silence while listening to the concert music and left our seats during the intermission before dessert was served. Julian introduced me to several acquaintances, including a few key people who made generous donations to the university.

"Dear Anna, how lovely to see you." Julian greeted a woman in a splendid charcoal Oscar de La Renta lace and tulle gown. Her auburn hair was perfectly styled in a French twist, and she dripped and dazzled in Chopard diamonds.

"Darling, you look incredibly handsome this evening," Anna purred. The temptress kissed Julian on the cheek, wiped the crimson lipstick off his skin, and caressed his handsome face. His lack of response threw her off, and she recoiled, sneering at me with venomous hostility as if I was to blame for his non-interest. She was right. I was the woman in red who held Julian's gaze captive that night.

"Who's this, Julian? A new pet?" Anna inquired, eyeing me up and down.

"Anna, this is my date, Sapphire Blake." Julian protectively placed one hand behind my back, rubbing it with assurance.

"How lovely, Julian! Lovely choice." She sniffed the air before walking away.

"She doesn't like me much," I pointed out.

"Clearly," Julian chuckled. "Anna's husband is one of the wealthiest men in Lester Harbor. He owns an engineering firm."

"Oh. What's the name of the firm?"

"Spear Energy."

"Oh, really? My dad works there."

"Small world."

We walked out to the balcony to get some fresh air. Julian leaned on the railing and gazed in sweet contentment at the river.

Over the past weeks, we had been meeting at our usual place at six o'clock every Tuesday. We'd start with dinner and conversation, followed by a stroll along the university greens to the car park. We would drive to Julian's place in his sleek, gray BMW convertible, and then shower together before we explored each other's bodies, where he would teach me new pleasures and delights. I learned how to use my mouth and tongue to give his cock pleasure, and he stimulated my senses with his fingers, oils, feathers, the finest chocolate sauce, and, of course, the art of cunnilingus. That was our ritual every Tuesday evening, and I woke up in his bed every Wednesday morning.

We celebrated his birthday in November—I learned that he was a Scorpio. Julian laughed when I told him that Scorpios' enigmatic nature made them incredibly seductive and beguiling.

"I don't believe in astrology, sweetheart," he responded, with a fever-inducing kiss.

I also understood that Julian was an affectionate giver to those he cared about. He began to buy me small, but expensive, gifts as tokens of fondness. The previous week, he'd surprised me with the famous Chanel Allure Eau de Parfum, a rich and fruity fragrance that was elegant and sweet. It was different from my usual daytime signature scent by Ralph Lauren, which represented a certain element of preppy freshness. In contrast, Chanel radiated a classy evening aroma of sensual femininity. At the concert dinner on Christmas Eve, I was cloaked in the fragrance of Chanel—it would be the only thing I would wear later that night.

After the dinner was over, I noticed an ethereal, tall goddess with long, ash-blonde hair standing up from her seat. She was draped in a show-stopping gold, hand-beaded gown with a plunging neckline meeting at the waist in a crystal-embellished buckle. I had never in my life seen a person more stunning than this woman, who commanded power and a high degree of authority. She looked at Julian and raised her eyebrows, a gesture that he returned by raising his champagne glass in a mock toast.

"Who's she?" I asked.

"She's the spirit of Christmas Past," Julian jested.

December 25, 1:00 a.m.

"It's time, love."

"I know."

"Are you ready?"

"Yes, Julian. I'm on the pill, and I am more than ready."

I was naked, facing Julian in his dimly lit bedroom. He stood in front of me, wearing nothing but a crisp, white, collared shirt. His erect penis thrust out of his shirt, which he started to unbutton after removing his cufflinks. The half-open shirt revealed a glimpse of broad, muscular shoulders and a smooth, masculine chest, which tapered down to a hard, tight abdomen. His eyes were a dilated sea of darkness, staring at me with animalistic lust, and his square jaw tightened as he gazed at my nudity.

"Tonight is different," Julian softly spoke, pulling me into a tight embrace and refusing to let go.

I played with the collar of his shirt while kissing his neck and tasting the spicy sweetness of his scent. I helped him unbutton his shirt, removing it and letting it slip unto the polished wooden floor. He mastered the art of seduction, pressing one hard, probing kiss on my lips before lifting his head.

"You're on heat," he murmured, as his fingers brushed past my mound and stroked the lips of my moist pussy.

"Only for you," I whispered, stroking his hard dick. I breathed in the strong, heady scent of his sex, then proceeded to work some magic on his testicles, cupping them with my hand as my fingers massaged the sensitive sac.

"*Sapphire*, my love," he moaned my name. "There is no gem like you."

My hand continued to explore him, and my fingers dug into his muscled thigh, moving deep under his balls. His cock responded with a twitch, while my index finger explored the area close to his anus.

"Oh, God, Saph. What are you doing to me?" Julian groaned loudly, then nipped the nape of my neck.

"I want to make love to you, Julian. Please make love to me," I urged.

"My treasure, you'll get plenty from this cock tonight." He grinned, bringing my face to his before he nurtured my lips with gentle kisses. "Come to bed with me," he coaxed, guiding me to lie down on the silky bed sheet after moving the soft duvet to one side.

Not a second passed before he was already on top of me, face-to-face.

"Kiss me, Julian. Kiss me," I begged, stroking his back with my nails. My legs parted as a welcoming gesture for him to take my body.

He bent his head, and his lips hotly greeted mine with ravenous passion. His kisses were a hungry man's plea, begging to be fed with my sweet affection. I was blind with explosive excitement which engulfed my entire body and soul in scorching flames. I felt immensely and deeply connected to this man.

"I need you so much, *Sapphire*." Julian's passion-glazed eyes pleaded with mine, while the smooth tip of his penis prodded my warm, wet entrance.

I nodded my head in trepidation and excitement.

"Take it, Julian. Take my virginity." I closed my eyes and clung tightly to him, silently praying that he would take all of me.

"Open your eyes, darling. I'll do my best to be tender with you," he whispered, as the head of his cock started to enter my core.

"Come to me, love." I kissed his jaw and bucked my hips, inviting him to push further.

His thick member pushed past the slick flesh of my center, sending a signal of sharp pain once it tore the hymen. I involuntarily let out a soft whimper and shivered from the impact of Julian's stinging invasion, clutching him tightly.

"Shh, the pain will pass, my love," he said, as he caressed my cheek, wiping away a stray tear that rolled down my left eye in response to the shock of the burn.

"Julian, it hurts," I cried softly.

"Would you like me to stop? Just say it, and I'll stop."

"No! Don't stop, Julian. Please keep going." I pressured his buttocks, signaling for him to continue as the pain *slowly* subsided.

He made a slight nod and proceeded to roll his hips into me, thrusting at first with gentle care, then pounding harder as I pulled him into me deeper. My body experienced a new world of pleasure with each thrust of his cock, which moved steadily and rhythmically inside me. Our lovemaking created a sea of heavenly ecstasy, and Julian was my drug.

"You're home, baby," I whispered, listening to Julian moan louder and breathe heavier with each thrust.

My nipples were hardened pebbles, and my pussy clenched his cock while an intoxicating feeling arose inside me, like euphoria spreading throughout my body. I turned my head, grabbed Julian's buttocks, and arched my back as my inner walls squeezed his cock with strong intensity.

"Julian!" I screamed, releasing an orgasmic explosion of tremendous force that ripped through me so deeply that my mind went blank.

Julian responded with a loud cry, and his body quivered as he ejaculated inside me. His arms tightened, and his body pulsated with mine before he collapsed into me. A moment later, he still clung onto me, refusing to let go, as if he was holding onto a lifebuoy in deep, stormy waters.

Julian Carpenter Richland was my first love. I became his on Christmas Day.

Julian
December 25, 9:00 a.m.

Waking up naked with an angel in my arms marked a wonderful start to Christmas Day.

"Merry Christmas, love." I kissed her sleeping head, breathing in her natural scent.

The woman was still fast asleep. I peered down and saw a light bloodstain on the bedsheet—evidence of her virginity lost. I sighed, dreaming of the events that had taken place just hours ago. My eyes traveled to the doors of my walk-in wardrobe. Behind those doors, on the second drawer to the left, was Sapphire's Christmas gift: a gold Cartier bracelet set with ten brilliant-cut diamonds totaling 0.21 carats. How I had done without this woman in my life was unfathomable. Sapphire was different.

I was falling.
Falling.
Falling.
In.
Love.

Chapter Thirteen
Symbiosis

Julian
March 15, the following year

"For your next assignment, you must demonstrate your knowledge on the current ideas on human evolution, ranging from the earliest hominins to the emergence of modern humans and their expansion."

"Sir, should we discuss key findings and theories on the hominin emergence, diversification, and dispersal?"

"Absolutely, Ben. This is a core subject, so if you want to pass archaeology, I expect you to consider human evolution in relation to the modern world and ask yourself whether we are still evolving."

"Sir—"

"Ben, I'm afraid we're out of time, but you can email me your questions. I'll see you all next week."

Ben Adeyemi was one of my best students, but he tended to ask questions when class ended. Shit, did they not understand that teachers wanted to go home after evening classes? In the next minute, I watched the students migrate then disperse outside the classroom. I was about to leave, when I heard a female voice call out my name.

"Professor Richland, I'm afraid I didn't quite understand the last part of the lecture," she purred, walking slowly and seductively toward me.

Damn those sexy legs and the poor fucking excuse of a miniskirt, which barely covered her smooth, creamy ass. I'd do anything to skim my fingers underneath and feel that wet, delicious cunt. I bet she didn't wear any panties.

"Send me an email. Class is over now," I replied, keeping it cool.

She still didn't take the hint. "Sir, I don't want to fail your class. Please help me." She toyed with my collar, slowly unbuttoning my shirt.

"Not here," I hissed. "Come see me in my office."

Her white, translucent top revealed she wore no bra, sending me dreams of handling her breasts. Thirty minutes later, we were naked in my office, with her face on my desk and her legs spread wide while I stood behind her, pounding her hard and fast.

"Oh my, sir, you're so fucking big! I want it so badly. I want you to give it to me hard!" she cried.

"How badly do you want it? Have you been good enough, love?"

"Oh, yes! Oh yes! Pump it in me, prof!"

I had her begging for me—this vixen of a woman. I pushed further into her, fucking her hard and giving her what she wanted until her inner muscles contracted, bringing forth the female orgasm. With a few more thrusts of my dick inside her, I joined her in releasing my tension, sending her all my love.

Cum dripped out of her raw, red pussy when I pulled out of her. Her firm, round ass was red with welts from a small whip that I'd used earlier that evening to teach her a lesson. I kept the whip, some rope, and a pair of handcuffs in the third drawer of my desk for special occasions. This definitely was a special occasion.

"Turn around. Let me see your fucking titties," I commanded.

The hot fox turned to face me, and her tits dangled, calling for me to play with them. I squeezed each tit, shaping them and forming them with my hands.

"Do you like this, darling?" I pulled and pinched her hard nipples while she stroked my cock.

"I love it, sir. I love it when you're rough."

"You can put the whip away now, love," I said. "And put your clothes back on in case any of my colleagues happen to knock on the door."

"Sure, honey," Saph replied.

Yeah, we did some role-playing from time to time. Saph occasionally attended one of my evening classes, sat in the back seat, and waited until I finished the lecture. She wore fuck-me-now outfits that made my cock hard and appreciative of her effort. We also had one rule for these occasions: never wear underwear.

Saph was fond of masks, blindfolds, and the whip, which brought her pained pleasure, and she encouraged me to smack her smooth bottom for some rough enjoyment. At home, she found joy in both tying me up and being tied up with rope.

"Let me know if it gets too rough for you, love," I always told her before we started our games.

"Of course I will. I'll say stop when I want you to stop."

She was my darling angel; I was a blessed man to have my celestial seraphim with all the light, ardor, and purity that was too good for the darkness of this cruel world.

Saturday, April 9

"Julian, what are you reading?"

"It's an article on symbiotic relationships, which refers to the interaction between two different organisms living in close physical association, typically to the advantage of both."

"Darling, I overheard a student say that you're a little too tough with your marking. Do any of them get an A?" Saph's eyes questioned mine.

"Rarely."

"Wow, you're tough."

"It's college, not a charity."

"Was Jessie a stellar student?"

"That's none of your business," I replied icily.

"I was just curious. Sorry for asking."

I sighed and rubbed my forehead. I didn't understand why the past needed to be excavated as if it was a human remain in a peat bog.

"Don't be sorry. Your curiosity and your desire to understand people are commendable. Jessie Caruso was not particularly sagacious, nor was she astute. She was clever in other matters. That's all I need to say."

"Cool. I was just curious," she replied.

I looked at her pretty oval face and wondered why she had been a virgin until I came along.

"Tell me about Cameron. Was he your first love?" I asked.

"No. I used to think he was, but I know now that wasn't the case. We both believed in saving ourselves for marriage, and he bought me a promise ring, saying he would ask me to marry him one day."

"And you went along with it? It sounds like child's play." I let slip a soft chuckle.

"I was young and so fucking naive," Saph responded. "Things are different now, and I'm less sure of anything these days because the world keeps changing."

"And yet, it remains the *same*," I refuted.

"What remains the same, Julian? The world is like a river, seemingly constant, yet the water keeps running. It is never the same water you see when you stand and watch it run."

"Water is water, air is air, and earth is earth. Just as we see that people are people. Different, yet the same. Look at the world, Saph. Open your eyes, love."

"Are we ready to go?" She picked up her beach bag.

"Yes, I'm ready."

Sapphire

By the time we arrived at North Point Beach, Vera was already there, resting on a beach chair next to another woman who had a large German Shepherd sleeping on the sand near her.

"Long time no see, Saph! I've hardly seen you at home after you started dating my brother." Vera greeted me with a cheeky grin.

"Well, consider it a donation from Julian to help us save costs on our water and electricity bills. We spend less, and he pays more," I joked, diffusing an unspoken conflict of feelings between Vera and myself.

Vera took the bait, relaxed, and laughed; however, Julian remained silent. A pair of lovely, tanned legs stretched out from the beach chair next to Vera. The mystery woman wore a black bikini, a pair of dark shades, and a wide-brimmed sun hat.

"Mom, there's someone I'd like you to meet," Julian announced.

The woman removed her sunglasses, and I was bedazzled. Wow. This was Frances Richland, the mother of my boyfriend. She looked terrific for a woman in her early fifties, with her enigmatic, dark eyes and long, wavy, caramel hair.

"Hello, dear." She sat up and smiled at me.

"I'm Sapphire Blake, and it's a pleasure to meet you, Mrs. Richland."

"Please, call me Frances. Sapphire is a very pretty name." Frances revealed a faded English accent, blended with the local tone of a long-term Lester Harbor resident.

"You can call me Saph," I responded.

The dog woke up, sniffed me, and excitedly placed its paw on my leg.

"Shh, Coby! It's a family friend." Frances hushed the dog, who barked with delight, before sitting down and staring at the ocean.

Julian grabbed two spare beach chairs, unfolded them, and stretched out on the one nearest to Vera. I sat on the other chair between Frances and Julian. I admired Julian's toned and tanned body, which glistened under the sun after we'd applied sunscreen on each other. His naked chest displayed masculinity in its finest form, and his board shorts hung low on his slim hips.

Vera cranked up the volume of her radio, which played beach lounge music, aggravating Julian.

"Vera, turn it down a notch," he reprimanded, slightly shaking his head in annoyance.

"Jules, don't be such a spoilsport!" Vera turned the volume down.

"*Nothing* ever changes. They've been like that since they were kids," Frances chuckled, putting her shades back on.

The afternoon went by quickly as we rested, chatted, drank cold drinks, and waded in the waves. I left Julian and Vera, who played with Coby near the water, to keep Frances company. She preferred to rest on the chair, absorbing the beach atmosphere. We stared at the rolling waves of the ocean in serene silence, then Frances broke the ice between us.

"My children think highly of you," she remarked. "Both Vera and Julian respect you a great deal."

"Thank you, Frances."

She removed her glasses and gazed at me.

"Julian is a man in love right now." The skin on the sides of her eyes creased as she smiled.

"Oh, I don't think so, Frances."

"Believe me, I know my son. I recognize his expression because it's the same look my late husband, Jasper, used to give me."

I looked at the siblings, who were now walking along the beach with Coby toward the lifeguard's hut.

"I don't know how much Julian told you about me," Frances said.

"He didn't tell me much."

"I'm not surprised. He doesn't say much because he's an introvert, like his father," Frances chuckled. "I'm an accountant, and my maiden name is Carpenter. My mother was from Portugal, and my father was from Bournemouth, not too far away from London, where I grew up. I met Jasper, who was visiting mutual friends thirty years ago, and we exchanged numbers."

Her face radiated with passion when she told me her story—about how she and Jasper met, married, and moved to Lester Harbor to start a family. "Jasper was a geophysicist, but his true passion was music. He played the piano at local concerts from time to time. I see so much of him in my children. Vera has his tenacity, and Julian has his kindness."

"They're both my best friends," I said.

"Tell me about yourself, Sapphire. Julian tells me that your parents are both engineers living north of the city."

"That's correct. My father, David, manages a major project at Spear Energy. My mother, Sylvia, works as a project engineer for another firm. They're both active members of Northern Lakes Baptist Church, where my dad leads the church council."

"Your parents seem to be both prominent and well respected, Saph."

"They are, I suppose. They tend to focus on appearances at times and forget that the rules of religion and society don't make you a better person. It's what comes from the heart that matters, and our actions speak louder than words," I sighed, hoping that Frances didn't think I was too outspoken.

"Well, in the Richland household, you are more than welcome to speak your mind, and we will try our best not to feed you with any propaganda." Frances grinned and reached out for my hand. I took her warm, slender hand and squeezed it with gentle affection.

"Oh look, they're coming back," she exclaimed, watching her children return to us.

I truly felt at home with Julian, Vera, and Frances. They were becoming my family.

Chapter Fourteen
Lust, Love and Hypocrisy

Sapphire
Saturday, April 23, 7:00 p.m.

I missed Vera, despite living with her. I was dating her brother, but I yearned to touch her soft skin, kiss her delicate lips, and play with her beautiful, silky hair. Her dark eyes were like Julian's, seductive and intense.

On the evening we decided to stay in and catch up as friends, Vera was a sex goddess in her navy-blue, lace negligee.

"Vera, I miss you. What if I'm like Julian? What if I'm polyamorous?" I asked, as we painted each other's nails in the living room.

"In this case, you can't have both, Saph. You chose my brother," she chuckled. "Besides, I promised Jules that I wouldn't touch you."

There she was, charming me with her seductive smiles and playful laughter, not fully aware of the effect she had on me.

"He still sees other people from time to time, like tonight," I declared.

Julian was out that evening, but he wouldn't disclose much of his private business.

"I'm sure you and Jules will come to some agreement if you wish to see anyone else. However, you have to trust me on this—he wouldn't want us gallivanting about like a pair of nude Lady Godivas behind his back."

"Oh?"

"Darling, I'm his sister, and he never liked sharing with me. When we were kids, I ditched the dolls for his cars, and believe me, that did not go down so well. After that, I had my own model car collection."

"I understand, Vera. Some good things must come to an end," I said, with a tone of sadness.

"In this case, yes, and we both know the reason for this. Firstly, I respect Jules. Secondly, you're in love with my brother, and you will *always* choose him over me. I need so much more than that, sweetie. I need exclusivity in a relationship."

I recalled how Vera used to kiss me, bringing an intoxicating comfort and a delicious sweetness. However, she was right. Deep inside, I wanted Julian more than anyone in the world. That night, I missed the spark that came with his kisses that warmed my soul with a *joie de vivre*, evoking the greatest joy of my spirit.

"Vera, Julian and I haven't talked about love," I revealed.

"Honey, Julian's yours. By the way, why hasn't he met your family yet?"

"I don't feel comfortable spending time with my parents. My father is a controlling man and my mother is weak. She goes along with everything he says, and it bothers me. I see her at church, but her conversations are pretentious, and her heart is empty."

"I'm sorry, but maybe she's hiding a great deal of pain beneath that mask," Vera speculated.

"Of course she is," I confirmed.

"On top of that, my parents and Cameron's parents are the best of friends. They still hope that he and I will reunite, get married, and be a happy family in their world. When I ended things with Cam nearly two years ago, my father was highly disappointed in me."

"Sheesh! Despite what Cameron did? No offense, but your dad sounds like a big dick. When you say he was disappointed in you, what do you mean, exactly?"

"Well, he lost his temper and told me I was making a grave mistake and that I would regret my decision. He also said I was turning into a heathen and that he struggled to pray for my troubled soul."

"How did you react to that?"

"I referred to Luke nineteen in the Bible, where people grumbled about Jesus going to the house of a sinner as a guest. I told Dad that Jesus preferred the sinners over the saints."

Vera snickered, and I responded with a giggle.

"I know it seems so ridiculous. Dad said I blew my chance when Cam started dating another girl from church. Truthfully, I was happy for Cam."

"Saph, why don't you bring Julian to church next Sunday? I dare you to shock the hell out of your parents. What's the worst that can happen? They might like him, for all you know."

I loved Vera's idea. What would be the worst that could happen?

Sunday, May 1

"People often confuse holiness with rules and expectations set by society," Pastor Lewis preached, while the congregation nodded their heads, ummed, and aahed in agreement.

Julian and I sat at the back, listening to the young pastor deliver his Sunday morning service to a full house at Northern Lakes Baptist Church.

My mother and father sat next to Cameron's parents in the front row, and my brother, Roland, stood with the rest of the choir near the podium. Cameron sat in the middle row with his new girlfriend, Charlene Chang.

"Now, why would we believe that God doesn't like variety and wants everything to be based on societal norms and expectations?" Pastor Lewis continued.

"I like this guy," Julian whispered, holding my hand.

"Me too. My dad and some of the council members are trying to get rid of him, but Pastor Lewis appeals to the younger generation," I confided.

"God doesn't need Christians who look like they've been baptized in sour grapes. I want you to ask yourself why you're doing what everyone else is doing. Instead, try living by what's true to your heart and enjoy life … maybe even get a tattoo or a piercing while you're at it!" Pastor Lewis concluded his sermon, eliciting cheers and claps.

After we sang the last song of the service, Julian and I stepped into the busy foyer, where a large gathering of people were chatting, drinking coffee, and eating snacks. My heart was beating rapidly out of pure nerves. Since Cameron, Julian was the first man I was about to introduce to my parents.

"Saph, you're looking well," Mom commented, when she came into the foyer. Her chin-length bob haircut perfectly framed her face, and her slim-fit designer dress suited her thin, wiry frame.

"Where's Dad?" I asked.

"He's still inside, chatting with a family who just joined the church. I see you brought a friend with you."

"Mom, this is Julian. Julian, this is my mother, Sylvia."

"It's a pleasure to meet you, ma'am." Julian shook Mom's hand.

Cameron and Charlene, who was a few years younger than us, came over to join our little gathering.

"Hi, I'm Cameron and this is my girlfriend, Charlene. You must be Julian. Saph mentioned you to me." Cameron shook Julian's hand.

"Professor Richland, I was in your introduction to archaeology class last semester," Charlene announced.

"I thought I recognized you," Julian replied.

"You're a tough marker, prof! You made my friend cry when she failed. I was just happy to pass," Charlene pointed out.

"So, you're a professor at the university. Tell me, Julian. Did you teach my daughter too?"

"No, she was not a student of mine."

"I see." Mom pursed her lips, then checked her watch.

"Good to see you, Saph. Nice to meet you, Julian," Cameron said, nudging his girlfriend to move on to the next group of people they would greet.

My dad, a silver-haired man with steel-blue eyes and a prominent jaw, walked over to us.

"Dad, this is Julian Richland."

Dad's eyes burned with fire at the sight of Julian, and his hands started to shake with fury. His face turned tomato-red and he was about to lose control. In all my life, I rarely saw my dad fired up with intense anger in public.

"Sapphire, I want you to stop seeing this man."

"But, Dad—"

"Julian, you are not welcome here!"

Julian

"Sapphire, Sylvia, please excuse Julian and myself. I'd like to have a private word with him," David said.

He then turned to me and said, "I would like to talk with you. Now."

I nodded and followed after David, who walked briskly toward one of the church offices. The man slammed the door, locked it, and faced me. I knew him. It didn't occur to me that this would be the same David

Blake I had seen at a few of Saira's secret soirées, which included doctors, lawyers, politicians, business executives, and senior managers of different firms. They had three things in common: money, upstanding positions in society, and the desire for dangerous sex.

"Keep away from my daughter! I swear, I will ruin you if you do not listen to me!" David bellowed.

"I suggest you tell her the truth about who you are before she finds out," I replied curtly.

"Will you tell her?"

"It's not my place to divulge family secrets."

"If you cared about her, you would stay away from her. I don't want her to get hurt."

"I love her, David."

"How much do women pay you these days? Remind me, Julian."

"That's none of your business." Saira had recently funded my research project through one of her businesses, in return for a few favors.

"You may be for sale, but my daughter isn't!" David yelled.

"Yet, you are more dangerous out of the two of us. You are Sapphire's father!" I accused.

"You're Saira's whore, and if she finds out you're in love, you'll endanger my daughter. Please keep away from her. It's not worth the trouble."

"How can you pretend to be a saint when you indulge yourself with countless women behind your family's back? I am honest with your daughter about the openness of our relationship. Have you been honest with your wife? Does she know what you do?"

"You keep your bloody mouth shut, boy!"

"You have no right to call me 'boy'! You can address me by my rightful name or title, whichever you prefer!"

"Julian, keep away from my daughter, or I will expose you and destroy your career with one snap of my fingers. I have a few buddies on the university board who owe me a few favors."

"You don't mean that."

He paused, then looked at me straight in the eyes. "Julian, if you love her, you'll do what's right for her. She needs a man who can give her stability, a family, and children. Let her go."

David's eyes softened. Despite his flaws, it appeared that he cared for his daughter. Perhaps he was right. Perhaps I should stay away and give Saph the opportunity in life she deserved—to truly be happy with a man who could offer her so much more.

"What do you say, Julian? Ruin my daughter and your career? Or leave her in peace and give her the chance she deserves in life? I offer you my peace and support if you choose the latter."

Saph deserved a better man. A good man. A man who could offer her more than the darkness that clouded my life. I couldn't face her at that point. I needed to be alone. Who was I fucking kidding all these months? Myself? Sapphire? My family?

At that point, my phone buzzed with a message. The sender? Saira Quinn.

"David, I have to go. Please tell Saph that something's come up."

The man nodded, then opened the door. I walked out of the room and left the church, refusing to turn back, no matter how much it killed me to leave her behind. Sapphire would be a remnant of the past. Her heart may hurt now, but one day she would thank me when she had that house with a white picket fence, two kids, and a loving husband who would come home to her every night.

That man was not me.

Chapter Fifteen
Hope is the Destroyer

Sapphire
Calligraphy, Tuesday, May 3

"Damn it, Julian, where are you?" I muttered to myself.

It was six-thirty, and it was highly unusual for Julian to be so late for our usual date. He was a punctual man, and something was not right. My father had refused to disclose what had gone on between him and Julian after the church service on Sunday. All he'd said was, "It's better if Julian makes himself scarce."

When I'd asked Dad if he knew Julian from before, he'd refused to say a word. Getting anything from him was like squeezing blood out of a rock. Nothing made sense to me anymore, because I had no fucking clue what was happening. I was not usually one to cry, but after calling Julian, leaving several messages, and not receiving one single response from him, I felt gutted. I was totally and utterly shattered into pieces. You know the feeling you get in your stomach when something is wrong before you receive terrible news? That was how I felt.

"There's got to be some bad blood between your father and Julian," Vera said, as I'd wiped my stray tears on Monday evening.

"Do you think he will turn up to our usual place tomorrow?" I'd asked.

"Go and wait for him there. If he shows up, it will be your opportunity to get the truth out of him," she suggested.

Tuesday evening came.

I waited. And waited. And waited. By seven o'clock, he still wasn't there. I sent him three text messages and called him four times while I sat at the café. I was persistent by nature, but there was only so much a woman could do before realizing that waiting there any longer was like trying to flog a dead dog to life.

Throughout the rest of the week, I felt numb. I couldn't feel anything anymore. Not even pain.

Then, on Friday evening, I received a message from Julian.

>Sorry, love, I've been tied up with a hectic schedule this week. Let's talk next Tuesday

That message was all it took to give me hope.

I also noticed a comment on his social media message board later that evening from DaydreamX67:

>Casino tomorrow night? 7 p.m. PW: Jeremiah.

Saturday, May 7, 7:00 p.m.

"Saph, are you sure you want to do this? Maybe it's best to wait until Tuesday to talk with him."

Vera crossed her arms when we arrived at the steps of the Lester Harbor's Grande Casino. She wore a sequin cocktail minidress and had styled her hair in thick, voluptuous curls.

"Vera, I need answers, and I'm not a patient woman. He owes me an explanation at the very least." I adjusted the silk strap of my shimmery black and gold wrap evening dress, which accentuated my slender curves.

"Whatever happens tonight with my brother, I want you to know one thing—I am here for you, okay?"

"Thanks, Vera. If he doesn't want to see me anymore, I want to hear it from him tonight. There's no point in waiting until Tuesday."

Ferraris, Porsches, Teslas, and Maseratis decorated the casino's entrance, where valet parking was offered. We stepped into the glamorous world of gaming action at the four-story atrium after having our ID cards checked by a security guard, who let us walk past the main doors.

The casino buzzed with all the glitz and glamor that money could buy at Lester Harbor. The baccarat, roulette, and blackjack gaming tables were surrounded by high rollers—men and women clad in their best suits and gowns. The atmosphere was flushed with the cheers and chatter of gamblers and partygoers. The bar brimmed with the thrill of live music and the clinks of champagne glasses.

Vera and I scanned and searched the ground floor for Julian, but alas, there was no sign of him. We went to the reception, where I asked the receptionist, whose badge read "Tony," if private functions were being held in one of the rooms.

"There's a special function on the top floor. However, it is an invite-only event," Tony confirmed.

PW: Jeremiah, I remembered the comment said.

Aha!

"That's the function I'm referring to. The password is Jeremiah," I replied.

"The function is in room 415 on the fourth floor, and you will need this keycard to get in. Would you need one or two cards?" He glanced at Vera.

"One should suffice," I said.

"Very well, then. Here you go. There's a deposit box near the door. You can drop the keycard in the box when you leave the party."

"Thanks, Tony."

"Enjoy your evening, ladies." Tony handed the keycard to me.

Vera was quiet until we reached the elevator. "I sure hope my brother is worth all the trouble we're going through." She exhaled loudly.

When we arrived on the fourth floor, my hands started to sweat and shake. My heart thumped faster when we reached room 415.

"Here goes!" I exclaimed, while Vera remained skeptical.

I inserted the keycard and opened the door.

Oh. My. God.

My eyes adjusted to the sight of an orgy-infested party that could have been hosted by Dionysus, the Greek god of wine, sex, ritual madness, and religious ecstasy. The room was filled with naked and half-naked people making out, having sex, drinking wine, snorting cocaine, smoking weed, dancing like mad, and eating an assortment of canapés. I saw three men and four women having group sex as I walked into the spacious penthouse-style room. It was decorated with expensive furniture and featured a large, open-air balcony that had a jacuzzi filled with hungry, nude lovers.

"Saph, let's go home," Vera suggested, looking concerned.

"No! I want to find him."

I walked on, and there he was. Julian sat on a red rococo lounge chair, with a drugged expression on his face. Despite that, he looked terrific in a crisp, white shirt, which was unbuttoned down to his navel. His hair was slicked back, and he had a slight stubble—he could have been on the cover of GQ, a men's fashion and lifestyle magazine.

He was not alone. A gorgeous woman with pristine ash-blonde hair, steel-gray eyes, scarlet-red lips, and pale skin stood behind him, caressing his body. It was the same woman from the Christmas Eve dinner Julian had taken me to the previous year.

A red-haired stripper wearing nothing but nipple tassels kissed Julian, taking his head to her breasts and rubbing them against his face. He returned her affection by removing a nipple tassel and kissing her naked nipple. He dipped one finger into her slit, removed it, and tasted the scent of her sex.

"Julian!" I was bewildered.

He simply stared at me. There was no smile. No sparkle in his eyes. No joy at all. His cold, dark eyes lacked emotion, and the muscles of his high cheekbones slightly twitched.

"Julian?" I repeated, feeling a flow of horrible trepidation surging from my gut to my knees.

"You have no business here," Julian replied coldly.

His eyes glared at mine, as if I was a stranger interrupting a lovers' tryst. The blonde woman slid her hand along Julian's back, sensually stroking and rubbing him. She simultaneously stared at me with a condescending kind of curiosity. Vera squeezed my hand, signaling for us to leave the party.

"Wait. Let me take a look at her," the woman commanded, angling her body slightly toward me.

"Saira, don't—" Julian began.

His eyes implored hers, while his hand lovingly stroked her free hand. It pained me a great deal to see my beloved surrendering his body and his feelings to another woman.

"No! I want to look at her," Saira objected.

"Come here, darling. I don't bite," she continued, while Julian's eyes shifted with unease.

I stepped forward, shoulders squared and head up, just as my parents taught me when standing up to bullies.

"My, you are a pretty young thing." She stroked my cheek in a blended state of amusement and curiosity.

I glanced around and saw another familiar face, which sent a thunderous shock to my spine.

My father!

The man I had doted on—no, looked up to—over the years had a naked woman in his arms, and that woman was not my mother. That woman couldn't be any older than me. My father was part of this bizarre, secret sex society. I suddenly felt dizzy and sick, while bitter bile rose up my throat. I held my breath, trying hard not to choke.

"DAD!" I screamed.

He looked away ashamedly, pretending not to know his daughter.

"Care to join us, sweet angel?" Saira asked.

"Julian's right." I glared at him in anger. "I have no business being here," I declared. "I have no business in your life. Nor do you in mine, Julian Richland."

I ran out of the place, blindly and as fast as I could, ignoring Vera calling out my name. I had to leave this life and start anew. Wicked Anxiety had won, and Lady Hope was gone. Maybe Wicked Anxiety was telling the truth, and Lady Hope was the wicked liar. I was in a place that was not physical—it was emotional and mental.

It was called hell.

Chapter Sixteen
Forgive Me, Love

Sapphire
Monday, May 9, 4:00 p.m.

I sat on a warm bench at Rose Park to meet my mother for a heart-to-heart chat. Anxiety gnawed at me like a plague of mice after I'd survived the shock of the hellish weekend. I'd ignored Julian's numerous calls and messages, because there was nothing he could say to make my pain go away at that point in time. As for my father—he may as well rot in hell with his feelings of shame if he had any. He'd made one call, which I'd missed after silencing my phone, and he'd failed to respond when I tried calling him back. One missed call was all it took for him to give up on me, and I knew him well. David Blake was a narcissist who rode in his Porsche with arrogance and pride as his companions. My brother, Roland, and I were mere trophies on his row of achievements.

"Sapphire." My mother approached me. She was immaculately dressed in a lime-green, silk blouse and a matching skirt. However, when she removed her Chanel sunglasses, her puffy, crimson, tear-stained eyes disclosed her pain.

"Mom. I'm so sorry," I began when she sat next to me. I tried to hug her, but she moved away. The woman was no fan of affection or physical comfort.

"I know everything, darling. Your father and I—"

"I hope to God that you're leaving him!" I spat, watching her flinch with discomfort.

"Excuse me? Leave your father? What kind of woman am I, Sapphire?" She drew fresh air in her lungs, clutching her chest as if I skewered her with blasphemy.

"MOM! He cheated on you!"

"I've forgiven him."

"What? What the fuck, Mom?"

"Watch your language, young lady! I didn't raise you to be low-class."

"How can you continue to live with him?"

"Him? What about you? You dirtied yourself and lowered your social status by losing your virginity to a male whore. What will you give your future husband now?"

"Don't belittle me or condescend me, Mother. You've chosen to stay with a man who has no respect for you or your children."

"Sapphire! Your father had high hopes for you to marry someone in our community. Someone like Cameron. Julian is wrong for you," my mother snarled.

"Stop right there. This isn't about Julian, Mom. This is about you, me, and my father, who is a two-faced, lying hypocrite! How can you stand there and watch him walk all over you and control your life? I don't belong in this family because I will never be like you or Dad."

"You are out of line, Sapphire! How dare you raise this in public?" my mother hissed, glancing at passersby around us.

I stood up and slung my handbag strap on my shoulder. Crucified by judgment, my injured soul evoked a piercing scream, sending her into a deafened state of shock. "You know what? Go fuck yourself, Mother! I don't give a shit about what other people think!"

"Your father was right. You are a lost cause." Mom stood up and pursed her lips with harsh disapproval.

"I am Sapphire Blake, love me or hate me. I will never be like you. You are weak, indecisive and pathetic! I've been silent all these years, and now I'm speaking out!" I towered over my diminutive mother.

"I don't know you at all. You are embarrassing yourself!" She sneered, shook her head, and folded her arms.

"I realize one thing now. I will never be the daughter you want because I will never be good enough for you. However, it is you and my father who were never good enough for me! You both let me down!"

"You disappoint me, Sapphire Audrey Blake. You may want to consider changing your surname, because you are no longer part of the Blake family."

"I will change my name in due time, because what you and that man gave me was false hope. There was no love, and our family was never truly real."

That afternoon marked the end of the farce that I once called "family."

Friday, May 27

"Let me in, Saph! Please!"

The door to our apartment was loaded with heavy banging.

"Go away, Julian!" I replied from inside.

"Please talk to me! I need to see you right now."

I couldn't bear the thought of seeing his face then. I was continuously reminded of Julian kissing the red-haired woman's nipple, tasting her vaginal juices, and being caressed by the woman he'd called Saira. My memory was haunted by his cold eyes and cruel words: "You have no business here."

"Saph, give me a chance to explain, darling!"

"I'm not your darling. You made it very clear the other night at the casino."

"I was trying to protect you."

"Hah! Protect me from whom? Cruella de Vil? The Wicked Witch of the East? Go home, Julian, and get some rest. I don't need any protecting."

"Honey, you should talk to him, please!" Vera pleaded. "He's standing outside, waiting."

"Well, he should have thought of that when he ghosted me, stood me up, and then told me that I had no business in his life!" I argued. I'd thought that I could make an open relationship work with the man, but after everything I had been through in the past few weeks, I couldn't take it anymore.

"I can understand why you shut your parents out, especially your dad, but—"

"I refuse to speak about Dad. Sure, he confessed to Mom, out of fear that I would tell her first. But do you know what she did?"

"I know, you told me before," Vera answered.

"I'll say it again. Mom turned a blind eye, as if nothing happened, and blamed me for creating the problem! Yes! She blamed me for making a big deal and bringing shame to the family! I swear, my mother must have undergone a lobotomy after she married Dad."

"I'm sorry, sweetie." Vera hugged me as tears rolled down my face.

"I feel such a disconnect from my family. My dad will never change, and now that I know the truth about him, I don't think I ever really knew the man." I breathed in, wiped my tears, and exhaled. "We were never a close family, you know. I always felt there was an emptiness when I was growing up. I'm sure Roland is feeling the same, but he rarely says much. He's a carbon copy of my mother."

"It's alright to cry. Let it out, Saph. Everything will be okay." Vera stroked my hair while I sobbed in her arms.

My phone started to ring again, and I switched it off. It was Julian calling. He then called Vera, who picked up the phone and spent the next few minutes explaining to him that he needed to give me space.

"What did he say?" I asked, after Vera put her phone away.

"He said he's on the way home now, but he wants to talk to you at some point because there's a reason for everything that's happened."

"Vera, right now, I'm not in a good place. I've been seeing a therapist to help me deal with the grieving process. I feel as if I've lost trust in humanity, especially regarding the two men who I love most in my life—Julian and my dad. It's been a double blow, so I hope you understand I need time."

"Alright, then. How much time do you need?"

"I can't quantify exactly how much I need at this point, but it will be a while." I sat up and frowned, staring at the brick wall.

"Saph, is there something you're not telling me?"

I bowed my head and sighed, then looked at Vera's espresso eyes, which pained me because they served as a reminder of Julian's.

"Vera, I'm thinking of moving out and renting a studio apartment on the other side of town."

"You WHAT?"

"I need my own space and time to think about what I'm doing with my life."

"How are you going to afford that? You barely make enough with your current jobs."

"Well, that's just it. I've been offered another job, a full-time position working for Senator McGrath as a public relations assistant." I smiled, as it was the one good thing that had happened to me in the past few weeks.

"Wow, that's great news, Saph! I'm so proud of you!"

"Thanks, Vera. I needed this lucky break."

Vera grinned at me, tucked a tendril of hair behind my right ear, and patted my shoulder.

"You're like a cat who lands on her feet. I know things are tough for you, but I know that you're going to be just fine. Call it instinct or intuition," she said.

"I feel the same too. I'm in a shitty place right now, but tomorrow has to be a better day. As for Julian, I don't think we'll get back together again. At least, not right now."

Julian
Tuesday, June 7, 8:00 a.m.

Saira's office was the last place I wanted to be, but something had to be done. The woman controlled politicians, lawyers, and businesses, and now she was attempting to control the university, through me, among others. She showed all the red-flag traits of a psychopath: lack of empathy, guilt, conscience, or remorse; superficial charm and glibness; shallow experiences of feelings or emotions; and a grandiose sense of their own worth.

Need I say more? Snakes like Saira were prevalent in the ranks of leadership, both in corporate life and in politics.

"Saira, let's make it brief. I want to get out of the deal. Completely."

"Really, Julian? Are you sure about that?" Saira slowly moved toward me, like a cobra in the grass ready to strike its victim. "My company provides generous funding to the university, which, may I add, played a key role in the success of your recent research project. You have staff who work for you, and their jobs depend on my generosity. Are you sure you want to back out of this deal?"

The woman dared to smile at me. The deal I had with Saira was meant to be an ad hoc arrangement; however, it had grown arms and legs with add-ons and clauses, turning me into a high-end male prostitute at her beck and call. The sex soirées had grown more frequent and dangerous, and I no longer wanted to be part of that lifestyle.

"I'm positive, Saira," I shot back. "No funding is worth toying with human lives. You know damn well that any woman I fell in love with would become a sacrificial lamb."

"Actually, Julian, I believe that *you* are the sacrificial lamb," Saira laughed, pouring a drink for herself. "Would you care for a drink? It's a fine brandy that finishes on a sweet note with a hint of cinnamon."

"I don't drink this early in the day," I scoffed, shaking my head in disgust.

"Your loss." Saira raised her eyebrows, swirled her glass, and took a swig of the alcohol.

"Just think, would you really choose your love for one insignificant citizen, who is practically a *nobody*, over a team of colleagues who have families to take care of and mouths to feed? Hmm? Their jobs depend on your decision."

Saira put her drink down and toyed with my collar, stroking her finger up and down my upper chest. I gently removed her finger from my body.

"And now that I know that David Blake is the father of your dear, precious angel, this becomes more interesting. Let me put it this way— David's career, family, and reputation are safe, as long as you keep playing by my rules."

That bloody witch!

Two can play that game.

"Do you think that you are the only one in Lester Harbor with power and influence? Your ex-husband, Alistair Scott, seems to be quite influential, I believe. Isn't he challenging you in court for full custody of Damian?"

Saira froze in panic and fear. "Have you spoken with him?"

Checkmate.

"Saira, let's just say that you aren't the only one with connections. I have enough evidence to provide to the judge and Alistair to convey that you are neither mentally nor emotionally available for your son," I spat.

"Don't you dare bring my son into this, you lying son of a bitch!"

"Oh, I believe you've already brought him into this by playing your games." I took Saira's glass of brandy into my hand and drank the remainder of the drink.

"Would you like me to make a list of ways I can meddle, Saira? Mmm?" I placed the brandy glass back on Saira's desk. "I want out, Saira. Completely. Bring your solicitor here at eight o'clock tomorrow morning, and we will put into writing the termination of our existing relationship. There will be no contact between you and me in the future."

"You, Julian, are a fucking bastard!"

"And you, Saira, are a fucking bitch."

I opened the glass office door and made my way out of the madhouse. I had tried to protect Sapphire from Saira, the destroyer, but my fear had got the better of me. Saira was well connected with Spear Energy and knew David through the sex club. When I'd discovered that David was Saph's father, I panicked. I was scared that if Saira found out that I was in love with David's daughter, all hell on earth would be unleashed, with David losing more than just his job. He would lose not only his reputation as a leading citizen of his local community but, most importantly, his family. Sapphire's family would have been destroyed.

I'd tried to forget Saph to protect her family. I was going to end our relationship, but she ended it on the night at the casino when I was playing the part of the playboy lover, the lothario. I was on morphine, an opiate that decreased the feeling of pain, so I wasn't thinking straight. However, all I could think of now was Saph. I ached to touch her smooth neck and her supple skin, and see her sapphire eyes. I yearned for the conversations we had about life, love, and the world. We had a deep connection that I'd never shared with another soul after my dad had died.

She'd brought light into my life, which was once nothing more than a dismal darkness. Now, I intended to do whatever it took to win her back. It would take time, I knew. She was my Helen, and I would wage war against Troy for her. It took Odysseus ten years to make the arduous and often-interrupted journey home to Ithaca. Let's hope that I would be more fortunate than Odysseus and come home to my beloved angel, my Sapphire, sooner than later.

Forgive me, love.

Chapter Seventeen
Missing Treasure

The light shines in the darkness and the darkness has not overcome it.
John 1:5, the Bible.

Julian
Tuesday, October 11

Dearest Sapphire,

It's been five months since I last saw you and I miss you. I pray that Vera delivers this letter directly into your warm hands.

I thought of you when you had your birthday last month. You are now twenty-four years old. I hope you received my birthday card, which I passed on to Vera last month, if you read it at all. If you had allowed me, I would have taken you to Paris or Rome to celebrate the day the world became lucky to have such a treasure as you. Right now, you are my missing treasure, my blue-eyed gem.

I thought of us when I watched the wind chase the fall leaves that October brings, swirling in an endless circle along the sidewalk outside *Calligraphy* last Tuesday.

On the Tuesday after the incident at the casino back in May, I waited for you at our usual place. After calling you and leaving unanswered messages, I wanted to explain everything. You never showed up on Tuesday, May 10. I understand why you refused to take my calls and return my messages. However, I hoped that there was a chance you would turn up for our usual date.

So, I waited for you again the following week. Again, you failed to come.

I waited each Tuesday after that, for a good few weeks, until I realized that I was chasing a dream gone by, just like the wind chasing the fall leaves. Yet, even now I still walk past the café at around six o-clock every Tuesday evening, hoping to see you through the glass window, sitting at our usual place. I cling onto dear hope, anticipating that you will be there reading a book or eating your favorite gluten-free jam doughnut. I miss you, my love.

I looked for you in the library and at the animal shelter, but you were gone.

"She left," they said. "She was offered another job."

I begged Vera to tell me where you were after you moved out of your apartment, but she blatantly refused, claiming that she'd sworn on our mother's soul never to tell me where you were. You have a good friend in my sister, because she kept her vow at her own brother's expense. Vera said you needed your space.

So, here I am on my own, waiting at our usual table at *Calligraphy*. While I hopelessly wait with my cup of coffee, I am writing to you in futile hope that you may take the time to respond to this letter.

I am sorry, Saph. I have written before, and I will write this again: I am sorry.

I am genuinely sorry for the Julian you saw at the casino. My sweet love, I cannot keep the truth behind my clandestine affair with Saira a secret from you anymore. You see, just as you have your secrets, I also have mine. The truth is, Saira and I had a business arrangement. I was seeing her on an ad hoc basis after our binding contract ended a few years ago. However, that arrangement turned sour, due to her growing demands and subliminal threats, in short.

Darling, you come from a family of wealth where you never had to beg, borrow, or steal to make ends meet. Your parents had a college fund for you, and you never had to ask for anything. I'm not blaming you for what happened. Not at all. In fact, it's quite the contrary. I blame myself for what I did to drive you out of my life. It started years ago when I was a broke student in a dire financial situation, with a hefty student loan that I would have to pay for most of my adult life.

That was just the iceberg on top of every single fucking bill that came my way, including bills that Vera or my mom needed help with paying. When my father died of cancer, we weren't left with much at all. Mom worked dog hours to make ends meet so we could have a roof over our heads and food on the table. A college fund was the last thing she could afford.

Maybe, in an ideal world, in a perfect utopian society, higher education would be free for all—offered as an equal opportunity and based on academic merit. Today, it seems that the children of society's cash kings and queens and oil barons benefit most from our current tertiary education system. I've grown up knowing that we live in an unfair world. Life is unjust, so I suck it up.

Saira came at a time when I needed her the most. She used my body, and in return, she provided financial means to pay for my college fees and to help me to live a life I could enjoy. I was a young sucker who was willing to learn all the secrets in the bedroom, so I became her professional lover.

Saph, I bedded countless women over the years, and never committed myself in an intimate and closed relationship. I never loved a woman before. During my high school years and before meeting Saira, sex was awkward and empty. While I found an intellectual connection with a few women, my heart failed to connect. Then there were those to whom my body responded in the most arousing and provoking manner, but my mind failed to connect with them.

When Saira came along, she showed me a new world of heightened sex. She was a clever woman with a sharp mind and a dominant personality. Sex was a sport, and I became rather well practiced in this type of physical activity, which yielded the greatest of pleasures. She opened the door to sordid sex soirées, where couples and singles mingled and engaged in all sorts of coital activities. I won't go into further detail on these wild affairs, pray your heart won't break more than it already has, but I need you to understand who I am.

I am not going to lie and say that I am a man of honor and decency. I am nothing like Cameron, who found his way back to a pure, reborn life in your church. Your family would prefer that you date men like Cameron, but I know you well enough to say boldly that they do *not* suit you. I believe that we are made for each other.

For all my flaws and darkened past, I am an honest man. You asked me once if I believed in God. I failed to answer at the time, as it is a deeply personal question. I will answer your question now—I do believe in God, just as the pagans believed in Jupiter, Ra, Odin, and Inti. Moreover, I believe that one does not need to show their glory in the churches to validate their belief in a god.

Faith is not based on fact, nor must it be taken as the truth. However, it is an intangible belief that I hold onto like a candle in the dark, may I be hopeless or not. Just as I hold onto my faith that your world and mine will collide again one day.

You intrigue me, Saph. You really do. I see a woman with wisdom and kindness, and I feel a deep connection with you when it comes to matters of the heart. I had never found such a woman before. That was until I met a precious gem who snuck into my bathroom once upon a time, curious to learn about the erotic pleasures a man like me could offer.

Remember that, Saph? You were a naughty girl, and I wanted to punish you for it in the most delightful and wicked ways. I wanted to bed you that day and every other day thereafter. I wanted to explore every part of your body, your mind, and your soul. I wanted to infiltrate you in your entirety, my *darling* Sapphire.

The incident at the casino occurred as a result of my subjection to Saira's demand for a male escort that evening. She needed a companion, which I reluctantly agreed to. She paid me handsomely by supporting my research project; however, I was unfulfilled. I ended my association with her in early June. I no longer need Saira in my life because I have found someone I need more.

That person is you.

I know that it is still early days between us, and I am learning to be a different kind of lover—one who has never experienced the full blossom of love. We are simply budding flowers, experimenting with the feelings that are fostered into a nurturing kind of love. I am sorry, again, for hurting you. I truly am. My words will not make you come back, but I do hope that you will return to me on your own accord. My appetite is lost to you.

Saph, I have a vested interest in you. What started as a companionship, in which I selfishly aimed to win your heart, has turned into a drama of errors where I am at fault, and it is me who has lost my heart to you.

Love me, Saph. Love me.

Don't answer me only in vain.

Don't doubt my feelings for you right now.

I want you to know one thing:

I, Julian Carpenter Richland, love you, Sapphire Audrey Blake.

I love you.

Yours,

Julian

Sapphire

"Take it, Saph. Julian begged me to make sure that you read it," Vera said, as she was leaving after stopping by my place for a cup of coffee and a quick catch-up.

I reluctantly took the white envelope from Vera's hand and thanked her for it.

"I'll see you next week, then. Good luck with the letter," Vera said.

"I'll be fine." I smiled and waved goodbye before closing the door.

I sat on the white IKEA sofa in my studio apartment, opened the letter and read the contents. I delved into the letter and read his words. Oh. My. God. It poured fresh honesty from Julian Carpenter Richland. Never in a million years did I expect this life-hardened playboy to tell me that he loved me. All his previous pleas and apologies were incomparable to the three words he revealed to me. *I love you.* However, in light of everything that had happened, I was still not yet ready to come to a truce with him.

I was in the process of making some changes in my life, and I needed to put myself first and foremost above everyone else. That included my parents, who I was no longer on speaking terms with, and Julian. It was time to tell the world to fuck off, because I deserved better. I walked into my bathroom, leaned over the sink, and stared at my reflection in the mirror. "Take care of yourself because no one else will," I muttered. Neither Lady Hope nor Wicked Anxiety were there. I was alone.

Saturday, October 15

"Are you sure you want to do this?" Kristoff asked.

"I'm positive." I nodded my head furiously.

"It's a radical change."

"I'm sick of not having change. Besides, it will grow again."

"Okay, Saph. It's your choice, so we will go with that style. I will give you highlights too," my hairdresser said, pointing at the cover of the magazine on my lap.

"Perfect, Kristoff. I trust you. My hair is in your hands."

The scissors snipped away curtains of wet, dark hair, which fell silently on the floor. Within minutes, the long locks were gone.

Chapter Eighteen
Hello, Professor

Sapphire
Saturday, March 11, five months later

"Come here, baby. Touch me."

"Darling, I'm going to yoga class in half an hour."

"Seriously? You couldn't sneak a little loving before you leave?"

I sighed, snuggled close to him, and breathed in his intoxicating scent.

"Come, let me touch you. That's it." He rubbed his thumb along my clitoris, stimulating it to wet heat.

I touched his bare chest and rubbed my hands along the hard muscles of his shoulder blades. His mysterious hazel eyes stared into mine. He was divine, like an ancient Olympian athlete.

Raphael Thomas was a beautiful angel with smooth, brown skin, gorgeous curls, and an air of confidence that appealed to many women. His parents were originally from Suriname and moved to Lester Harbor nearly thirty years ago. We worked closely together in Senator Paul McGrath's office and had started dating a few weeks back. As Paul's principal advisor, Raphael was an astute man who knew the ins and outs of politics and business.

Vera knew Raphael from law school and warned me to be wary of lawyers who delved into politics. I believed her and took her advice, but still allowed myself to have fun along the way. As for my family, I'd returned to church last week and sat in the back row during the service. I spoke with my mother and brother after the service, but I ignored my father. I would never forget when the prick pretended he didn't know me at the sex party, so why the heck would I acknowledge him at his church party?

He still led the church council and continued his relentless pursuit to get rid of Pastor Peter Lewis, the young and enthusiastic preacher who was too radical for my dad, the hypocrite. Mom invited me to dinner when my father was out of town or working late. That was the only time I felt comfortable visiting my old family home. I could not forgive my father for the pain he caused—it was a sharp sting that hurt like hell.

As for Julian, Vera said he was dating again. Good for him. I'd learned to forgive Julian, but I'd never forgotten the way he'd treated me. It was a case of being once bitten, twice shy. It was good to be dating again, and I was glad to have met Raphael. He would never replace Julian, but I had to move on.

"Raphael, you should go. You know how to find your way out," I hinted, kissing the angel's lips.

Fifteen minutes later, I stared at myself in the bathroom mirror, then looked down at the small wastebasket near the sink. A used condom and some tissues occupied the container, reminding me of my nocturnal activities with Raphael.

There's no use crying over spilled milk. Lady Hope stood by me, scolding me to move on.

I sighed and turned on the shower faucet, before stepping under the water for a wash. "Oh, I'm not crying," I muttered, holding back my emotions. My period was coming soon, hence the full swing of moods.

Yet, I felt empty—Julian's absence left a gaping hole in my heart, and neither man nor angel could replace that emptiness.

Monday, March 13

"Saph, McGrath wants you in his office." Raphael gently tapped my shoulder.

"Sure. What kind of mood is Paul in today?" My boss was a drama queen when he had his bad days.

"He's chirpy."

"Chirpy? I guess that's good." I ran my hand across my brow, pretending to wipe off nervous sweat.

Raphael chuckled and lightly stroked my arm.

"Paul, did you want to see me?" I walked into the senator's office, which smelled of fresh paint.

"Yes, Saph. Please take a seat."

I sat on one of the armchairs facing his desk, opened my notebook, and was ready to start jotting down notes.

"I've decided to donate to Montville State University's archaeology department for the excellent work they've been doing. I want you to write a press release on this," Paul announced.

The archaeology department. That was Julian's territory.

"Sure, I can do that," I said. "I'll draft something up, put in a few quotes, which I'll need you to review, and I'll need to contact someone from the university to get a few quotes from them, so we have a well-rounded media release."

"Precisely. I have a name for you. He's a young professor who plays a key role in the department. Don't get offended if he comes across as arrogant and aloof—he's exceptionally bright."

"What's his name?"

"Professor Richland. Julian Richland."

I froze.

"Oh."

My hand started shaking so much that I couldn't hold my pen any longer. It slipped from my fingers to the ground, and I picked it up.

"Is everything alright? You don't look well."

"Oh, it's probably my low blood sugar level. I just need a snack or fruit and some water. I'll be fine after that," I reassured my boss.

"Good. Now, the second thing I require of you is to accompany me to a special dinner for this fundraiser and get a few photos of myself, some local business leaders, and the professor."

"Sure."

"You can introduce yourself to him at the dinner and interview him after that."

"When and where is the dinner?"

"The dinner will be at Saint Augustine's Place at the university campus at seven o'clock on Friday."

"This Friday?"

"Am I referring to any other Friday?"

"Got it, Paul." I stood from the chair and started making my way out of the senator's office.

"Saph? Make sure you get some rest. I want you in good shape on Friday evening."

"Sure."

Holy fucking shit.

Friday, March 17, 7:00 p.m.

Raphael and I arrived together at the fundraiser dinner at Saint Augustine's Place. Built in the nineteenth century, it retained its original grandeur and housed nationally renowned paintings. After a few minutes of mingling with the crowd, I took photos of Paul and Raphael with prominent business leaders. I knew it was only a matter of time before I would face Julian.

Sure enough, I spotted him on the other side of the crowded room. The professor wore an immaculately tailored navy-blue suit, paired with a crisp white shirt and a subtle blue tie with a gold lapel pin. Julian's signature stubble was neatly groomed, and not a hair on his head was out of place. He was the devil in disguise.

Of course, he was not alone. A beautiful Eurasian woman stood close to him, and her hips touched his. His left arm snaked around her waist, and his fingers gently stroked her rib repetitively. The woman could have been on the cover of *Sports Illustrated* magazine.

Then it happened. Our eyes locked across the room, arousing Julian's senses. I stood there, a frozen statue, as he made his way toward me, bringing his date with him.

"Professor Richland, it's good to see you again," Paul said, shaking Julian's hand.

"Likewise," Julian replied, gazing at my black satin dress, before looking at the senator.

"Professor, I would like to introduce you to my advisor, Raphael Thomas, and my assistant, Sapphire Blake," Paul announced.

"Pleasure to meet you." Raphael shook hands with Julian, who seemed repulsed at the sight of Raphael's body angling close to mine.

"Raphael will discuss the details of the donation with you later, Julian. Sapphire is the one I was telling you about on the phone. She'll write the media release and interview you for a few quotes to go in the release."

Julian took my hand. He tilted it, so my palm faced flat down, then lifted my hand toward his lips.

"Saph," he murmured, planting a gentle kiss on my hand. "As usual, you take my breath away."

"Excuse me, do you know each other?" Julian's date interrupted.

Paul looked gobsmacked, as if he had just witnessed a man dousing himself on fire.

Julian cleared his throat, then announced, "Sapphire, gentlemen, this is Anita Weber."

"Lovely to meet you. I've never met a senator before," she drawled, clearly blinded by Paul's status.

Paul responded with enthusiasm, as his eyes lit up with delight and amusement. Julian and I grinned at each other, and it hit me. Our flame had never blown out in the darkness. It had only flickered and dimmed, but now it sparked brighter than it had for a long time.

Raphael interrupted our implicit declaration of feelings. "Saph, I didn't know that you and the professor know each other."

"Oh, we have history together," Julian teased, letting slip a naughty smile.

Paul looked at me with surprise, then revealed a lopsided grin.

"Saph, I see you're a keeper of secrets," he declared.

I cleared my throat to break up the awkward silence that followed Paul's statement.

"Paul and Julian, I think now would be a good time for me to take some photos of you together for the press release," I said.

A few minutes later, after the photos were taken, Julian readjusted his tie, while Anita zoned in on the senator.

"Senator McGrath, did you know that we have a resident artist who recently showcased some of his art in the building?" Anita asked, gently placing one hand on his arm.

"No, I was not aware of that." Paul grinned, eagerly receptive to Anita's gesture.

"If you like, I can show you some of his work," she suggested, smiling coyly.

"I'd like that very much," he flirted back, allowing her to link her arm with his.

Julian chuckled, watching them walk away. I joined him in the gentle laughter, amused at how quickly his date moved on from one man to another.

"It's called power," Julian responded, as if he read my mind.

"Where did you find her?" I snickered, not holding back on my comment.

Julian raised one eyebrow and smirked.

"Julian, I don't think I made myself clear. Saph is my girlfriend," Raphael butted in.

I was taken aback by Raphael's bold lie, but Julian's face began to storm and rage with crimson darkness. Upon hearing Raphael's words, he turned away and bolted in anger without saying goodbye, leaving me to face Raphael alone.

"Why the fuck did you say that? You're a bullshit artist!" I raised my voice.

"The guy's a player, Saph. Earlier this evening, I overheard someone say he fucks and chucks the women he dates," Raphael answered.

"You do not get any say over my life, Raphael!" I stormed off, following Julian.

***

"JULIAN! Stop!" I ran after him as he quickly marched across the university lawn.

He kept walking, ignoring my plea.

I lifted the hem of my dress, removed my heels, and sprinted behind him until we were on the other side of the campus lawn, far away from Saint Augustine's Place. We were surrounded by birch trees, trimmed hedges, and a dimly lit area that homed a stone bench.

"Damn it, Julian! Raphael is NOT my boyfriend!" I yelled.

There. That got him to stop walking.

"Then what is he to you?"

"What is Anita to you?" I fought fire with fire.

"I barely know the woman. We met a few weeks ago, we fucked, and she's here tonight. End of story." He shrugged his shoulders, not giving a shit about his date.

Julian's dark-brown eyes fixated on mine, then he frowned.

"You cut your hair."

"I have. People change, Julian, like running water in a flowing river. I've changed."

"Yet, you are still the same. Water is water."

"Raphael and I were never serious."

"Are you sleeping with him? Tell me, Saph, does he make you cum? Does he love you the way I do?"

"He satisfies me."

"Sure."

"Julian, don't give me that look."

"What look?"

"The grimace that you're pulling right now."

"Do you know how pissed I am?"

"Julian." I touched his arm, but he winced in pain.

"Do you know what I did with Saira last year? I fucking went to her office to end it with her! I did it for us because I love you! You can't put a price on love, angel."

Julian removed his jacket, loosened his tie, and rolled up his sleeves. I couldn't help but notice the bulge of his muscles under his shirt.

"Why are you staring at me that way?" His eyes softened.

"I–uh—" I started to stutter with my words.

"You want me." Julian's mischievous eyes sparkled with delight. He raised his left eyebrow, and the left corner of his mouth began to reveal a sly grin.

I moved closer, breathing in his musky cologne.

"I do," I admitted, gazing straight into his honest eyes.

"I want you, too. God, Saph, you have no idea how much I've missed you. I love you."

He ran his hands through my hair, pulling it slightly, but not with force.

"I never forgot you," he murmured. "Saph, I want to give you the world."

He pulled me into a tight embrace, rubbing his hands up and down my lower back. He then grabbed my buttocks, clenching them with his grip. I felt the hardness of his erection push hard against my pelvis as he kissed me deeply, his assertive tongue dominantly toying with mine.

"Fuck, I want to take you right now," he growled.

"Take me back to your place," I suggested.

I undid his belt, delved inside his pants, and massaged his hard, naked cock. He groaned as my thumb rubbed his cock's smooth head.

"Let's get out of here."

Chapter Nineteen
Aphrodisiac of Pleasure and Pain

Sapphire
Julian's apartment

Julian let out a muffled yelp out of shock as I smacked his buttocks with a leather paddle.

"Do you want more, baby? Tell me you want more!" I ordered him.

His hands and feet were tied with rope, and a silicone ball gag silenced his mouth.

He nodded his head frantically.

Whack!

"Mmff!"

WHACK!

One single tear ran down his face as he stared at my bare breasts.

"Do you still want more, or are you satisfied with what you've got?" The corners of my mouth turned into an evil grin.

He was on his knees by his bed, and I walked around him, ruffled his hair and stroked his beautiful jaw. His cock was erect, pointing upward in my direction.

You're in control, Saph. Make him sweat bullets. Wicked Anxiety stood by Julian, stroking the red marks on his lower back and ass.

He's anxious, and he's begging for your love. You're doing well. She slyly smiled at me, then saucily sauntered out of the room.

The man was between heaven and hell, experiencing the pleasure and pain of a half-naked woman teasing him mercilessly and relentlessly. I placed the paddle on the bed and picked up the key to the chastity belt, which was the only item of clothing I had on.

"You'll have to come and get it," I mocked, walking away from him.

"Mmm!" Julian whimpered for more, but I was not going easy on him. I turned to face him, dangling the key in front of his face.

"What if... I threw away the key?" I taunted him, stepping closer.

"Mmm!" Julian furiously shook his head as I patted it.

He tried to reach out for the key with his tied hands, but I stepped back, holding it high.

"No! You've been a bad boy, Julian." I grinned wickedly.

I removed my black lace masquerade mask and threw it on the floor. I also tossed the key on the ground, watching Julian's eyes grow wider. He quickly scrambled to retrieve the key, and I rewarded him by ungagging him and untying the rope from his hands and feet.

"You shouldn't have done that, you naughty girl!" His lips exposed a wicked smirk.

It only took seconds for Julian to seize my body, wrap his arms tightly around me so I couldn't escape, and unlock the chastity belt, which fell to the ground. The man was much stronger than me, so it didn't take much force for him to dominate this lovers' battleground. He threw me on the bed, face down, and rubbed his body on top of me. I felt his hardness grinding against my ass cheeks, and his warm, muscled frame encapsulating mine.

"I've got you, love. You're mine for as long as I have you," he growled, nipping my earlobes.

Julian was now in control. There was no mildness in the way he explored my wet clit with his fingers. There was only hunger driven with madness, accompanied by lust and desire. One finger in. One finger out. Two fingers in. Two fingers out. I gasped at the feel of Julian's long, experienced fingers dipping in and out of me with dexterity and finesse, causing a flush of slippery fluid to squirt out of my vagina. I felt the hot breath of his mouth on my neck and face. He tightened his grip on me, while his dick explored the outer rim of my anus, working its way to my wet pussy. He spread my legs wide on the bed and, without warning, his cock made its rough invasion, pushing hastily inside me. He moved rapidly, gripping the side of my left hip with one hand and stimulating my clit with the other.

"Does my cock feel good inside you, love?"

"Yes!"

He thrust fast, hard, and deep, punishing me with each animalistic movement. He grunted louder and rocked into my body faster, while soft moans escaped from my lips. There was no tenderness, and there was no gentleness. There was only carnal pleasure heightened by the sparks of pain.

"Do you want to slow down, baby?" I whispered.

"No."

He kissed my mouth deeply, prolonging the passion with his wicked tongue, which tangled with mine. He released the kiss from my mouth, and his lips worked along my neck as he continued thrusting hard.

"Do you still want another man's cock in you?" He breathed into my ear. He nipped the nape of my neck, then ruthlessly sucked on my skin while grabbing my hair.

"Oww!"

"Do you?"

"No."

"Tell me. Say it loud."

"I never want another man's cock again."

"Tell me what you want, Saph. Tell me."

"I want your cock. Only yours."

"Good girl. That's it. Good girl."

He pushed his cock harder and deeper, taking the lovemaking to a new speed until I could no longer control the exhilaration that was building inside me.

"Did you miss my cock? Did you miss me?"

"Yes! Oh, yes!"

My breathing quickened, and delirium washed over my body, sending me into an elevated state of nirvana.

"Yes! Oh, Julian! Julian!" I cried, feeling the familiar surge of intensified pleasure take over me when I felt his cock stiffen and release inside me.

He shouted my name over and over, before slowing down and whispering into my ear, "You are an angel."

The next day, 9:00 a.m.

"What are you thinking of, darling?" I was resting in Julian's bed, by his side, toying with his brown hair.

"I think that we're well matched," Julian laughed, revealing his white teeth. He turned to me, propped himself up on his elbow, and stared at my face. "Saph, I enjoyed the night."

Must all good things come to an end?

"What's going to happen now?" I needed clarity.

"What now? Well, you can start by making up for the time we lost."

"I guess we have a lot of catching up to do."

"We certainly do."

"Julian, I need to get a few quotes from you for this press release I'm doing for Paul about his donation to the archaeology department. Can you help me?"

"Sure, love. Consider it done. Send me the draft press release on Monday, and I'll add my quotes."

"Paul said you would be a tough one to work with," I laughed softly.

"I can be tough. I can be gentle too." Julian's hand fondled my breasts, then continued south, giving my pussy a gentle massage.

"So, here we are." I smiled, gliding my fingers up and down his shoulder and arm.

Interrupting our lazy Saturday morning, my cell phone rang and vibrated on Julian's bedside table. I reached for it and saw Raphael's name show up on the caller ID.

"Shit," I muttered, silencing my phone.

"Raphael, huh?" Julian's face tightened with pain.

"It's not important," I reassured him. I tried to soothe him with a stroke of my fingers to his hand, but he flinched, moving away. "Julian, he's not important to me."

"Why the fuck is he calling you now?"

"Does it matter?" Julian sat up and perched himself on one side of the bed.

"Julian! What's going on with you?"

The man I knew before was a hedonist who enjoyed the pleasure of an open relationship. The man who faced me now was possessive and jealous. Something had changed.

"I'm going to shower now." He stood up.

"I need to go home, Julian. I'm going to call a cab," I called out, watching the muscles of his back and his firm ass move as he walked toward the bathroom.

"Sure. Go back to Raphael."

I put my panties and last night's dress on and picked up my stuff. He was about to disappear into the bathroom when I yelled, "So that's it, huh?" He stopped, turned, and looked at me. "See you around, Julian. Last night was fun while it lasted," I scoffed, shaking my head.

His eyes softened, and his facial muscles relaxed. "No ... I'm sorry, love. I'm just a jealous guy."

Now, that just cracked me up. I inadvertently burst into laughter after hearing those amusing words spill out of this playboy's mouth. "Jealous? *You?* The Julian Carpenter Richland, who doesn't 'do' closed relationships?"

He nodded his head, admitting the truth. Oh, my God. I walked up to him, planted a kiss on his mouth, and nuzzled up to his neck, breathing in his natural, masculine scent.

"God, you're so addictive, Julian."

"Witch."

"Casanova."

"Fuck, you're intoxicating." Julian kissed my jawline. His eyes were drunk with debauched lust.

"I think we need to talk later. We don't need to make any decisions now, but we need to clear the air. What are your thoughts?" I asked.

"Saph, I want to see you again." He embraced me with his warm, naked body, and scorched my mouth with a burning kiss. "I'll do anything for you, love." His voice lowered. "Just don't shut me out. Don't ignore me."

"I won't ignore you, Julian. I won't shut you out. I have to go because I have a yoga class soon, but I will make sure that you *always* know where to find me."

He loosened his grip, reluctantly letting me go.

"Saph?" he called out, as I headed out of his apartment.

"Yes?" I turned my shoulder and glanced at him.

"I never forgot you."

"Number 21B, Cherry Street, Texas Square. That's where I live." I smiled like a Cheshire cat, satisfied with the events that occurred in the last twelve hours.

Before I left his apartment, I turned back and saw Julian grinning widely. That face glowed with satisfaction and happiness. Julian was a man in love. I felt a strong love for him too.

Chapter Twenty
Seduced by a Vixen

Sapphire
Calligraphy, Sunday morning

It had been a while since I'd enjoyed a cup of coffee at *Calligraphy*. I was in the neighborhood, dropping off some overdue library books I forgot to return months ago. I sat by the window, sipping a cappuccino while warming up to the natural sunlight that shone through the large windows. The strong aroma of rich coffee, blended with the papery scent of old books, infiltrated the café air. Listening to the familiar sound of coffee grinding, I closed my eyes, breathed in, and exhaled, feeling blissful and indulgent. It had been nearly two days since Julian had royally fucked me, and I was still on cloud nine.

"Saph, it's been ages since I've seen you here," Rosie's voice chimed, breaking my silent meditation.

I opened my eyes.

"Here's your fruit salad, and it's carefully prepared in a wheat-free environment," she assured me. She knew about my severe wheat allergy and took care to ensure my food was safe to eat.

"Thanks, Rosie. How have you been?" Over time, we had grown to know one another, often chatting whenever I visited *Calligraphy*. She was someone I could now call a friend.

"It just keeps getting busier, but Sundays are usually our quiet days."

"Great! Sit here with me for a bit, if you've got a minute or two." I offered the chair next to me.

"I suppose a minute won't hurt, and it's not busy right now." Rosie pulled the chair over and sat by my side. "So, are you still avoiding Julian? He was here every Tuesday for a while last year. No doubt, he came by looking for you."

Rosie's warm smile and sparkling eyes said it all. Julian was a hunter who spent months prowling for his lost prey.

"Uh, yeah. About that. We're picking up where we left off," I admitted, cheeks blushing.

"He's a nice fellow. Smart and good looking too. I bet he's great in the sack."

"He's one of a kind."

Rosie's eyes targeted my neck. "Hey, you've got some pretty big hickeys. Are they from Julian?"

"The one and only. As I said—"

"Julian's one of a kind," Rosie chimed, finishing my sentence.

We both laughed simultaneously. However, I noticed a glint of sadness in Rosie's sweet eyes.

"How's Evan, Rosie?"

"We broke up last month. It's been rough, but each day gets better."

"I'm sorry to hear that."

"Oh, I'm not." Rosie leaned closer and softly said, "The sex was pretty ordinary."

"Oh?"

"I never had an orgasm."

"Rosie!" My eyes shot up like fireworks lighting the night sky.

"Shh! I don't want anyone else to know."

"Are you telling me you've never had an orgasm in your life?"

Rosie nodded her head slowly, lowering her eyes.

"Even before Evan?"

"Uhm, hmm."

"Shit." I shook my head.

"Yeah, I know. It's bad, right?"

Rosie was beautiful. She had curves in all the right places, smooth cocoa skin, gorgeous jet-black hair, and seductive doe eyes that would make an army of soldiers bend on their knees at her command. I remembered Julian watching her with a piqued interest when we had our Tuesday dates at the café. He was attracted to her. I suddenly had an idea. I was curious and wanted to explore uncharted waters in my world.

"Rosie, do you think Julian is handsome? I've got an open mind, so whatever you say won't upset me."

"Uhm, yeah. I think he's an attractive guy," she revealed with caution.

"How would you feel if he gave you your first orgasm?"

Rosie looked up, and her eyes widened with excitement. "Are you okay with that?"

"Consider it a little gift from Julian and me." I grinned, eager to try something new.

Julian
21B Cherry Street, Sunday, 6:00 p.m.

"Julian!"

Only a minute ago, I'd rung Saph's doorbell, and she had just opened the door, reacting to my presence with startled curiosity.

"I wanted to surprise you." I gazed at my angel's oval face and wide sapphire-blue eyes.

She was braless, in a sheer, loose tank top and tiny denim shorts. I wondered if she had any panties on. Giant love bites decorated her delicate neck, matching the colors of soft pink, cerise, and red in the round bouquet of mixed roses that I gave her.

"Wow, the roses are beautiful! Come inside," she invited, taking the flowers.

"With pleasure," I replied, grinning at the woman of my life before entering her apartment.

"I bought you another gift. It's a book called *The Portable Machiavelli*, featuring a collection of works by Niccolò Machiavelli." I handed her the paperback.

"Thank you, Julian! I love your taste in books," the vixen purred.

"People are strong when united. It's in chapter fifty-seven in *The Discourses*," I said.

She returned my comment with a coy smile, causing my cock to harden. Fuck, I wanted to bend her over and give one of her holes a meaty welcome.

"You're looking at me as if I'm naked," she teased.

"God, you're so fucking hot." I pulled her into me and kissed her soft, pink lips. I'd missed my angel.

"Let me put the flowers and book away," she whispered.

Reluctantly letting her go, I checked out the curve of her ass as her long, creamy legs pranced to the open-plan kitchen. I felt the fabric of my jeans restrain my stiff cock. I followed behind her, then placed my hands around her waist, feeling the warmth of her slender shape. A few minutes later, the roses were scattered on her kitchen bench, and our clothes were strewn all over the tiny apartment. I pounded hard into my woman, on all fours on the floor, holding onto her naked hips.

"Fuck me hard, Julian," she cried, begging me not to stop as I continued slamming deep inside her.

"That's it. Talk dirty to me, baby," I coaxed, gripping her hard.

"I love your fucking dick! I think of your big dick riding my tight pussy when I touch myself," she cried.

"Fuck, Saph. I fucking miss you so much. I'm blind," I whispered into her ear, giving her smooth lobe a little nip and lick.

The only other sounds in the apartment were of my flesh slapping into hers and our heavy breathing as I fucked her tight, moist, and warm pussy. Saph's breathing became heavier, and her whimpers grew louder with each thrust I gave her, until we were ready to unleash our combined ecstasy.

"I'm so close to coming," Saph moaned.

Then I felt it. The walls of her sex tightened and squeezed my cock, milking its cum, which spread inside her.

"Fuck me, Julian! Fuck me!" she screamed, not giving a damn if the neighborhood could hear us.

"I love you, Saph!" I shouted, spilling what was left of my release.

A few seconds passed as we caught up on our breathing. I slowly withdrew from her and watched my seed spill out. My index finger circled her swollen, pretty pussy, and pushed inside, returning some of my cum into her.

"Do you love me, Saph? Do you?" I continued fingering her.

"Yes, Julian. I love you more than you know."

There. She'd confirmed it. My sweet angel loved me back. I pictured her pregnant with my child—my primal urge to start a family with her grew stronger over time. I wanted that house with a white picket fence. Saph would make an incredible mother one day, and I planned to be there with her. It felt so fucking natural to make Sapphire Blake a permanent part of my life.

"I love you so much, Saph. So fucking much."

"Julian, do you think that we could—"

"Don't think. Feel. Feel what we have."

One hour later

Saph and I relaxed and enjoyed our home-cooked dinner on a plaid picnic blanket on the rooftop terrace on the top floor of her apartment building. The place was lit with oriental lanterns and boasted a grand view of the city lights under the night sky.

"Julian, this risotto tastes divine!" Saph dug into the tasty rice meal I'd prepared post-sex. It was flavored with virgin olive oil, shallots, parmesan cheese, chicken, and mushrooms.

"Would you like some wine with that? I have right here a bottle of Pinot Grigio from your fridge and two glasses."

"Oh, yes, please!" Saph's eyes lit up like two blue flames dancing with delight as I unscrewed the bottle and poured the white wine into the glasses.

After handing a glass to her, I swirled mine, inhaled the spicy, lighter-bodied bouquet, then indulged in a sip of the Italian wine.

"This is simply gorgeous," Saph gasped, after trying the wine and taking another bite of her meal.

My heart beat rapidly. I was weak in the knees, and vulnerable as hell, just being with this ethereal nymph.

"Fuck," I muttered, running my hand through my hair.

"What?" Saph asked. "Did I say something wrong?"

"No. Not at all." I shook my head. I stroked her back gently and felt her body shiver in response. "Is everything okay, love?"

"Julian, this means something to me. You've done everything to make me feel right at home with you." She beamed a radiant smile that sent waves of excitement to my chest. "Julian, I want to try something."

"Anything for you, love."

"Do you remember Rosie from the café?"

"Yeah …" I remembered the pretty waitress with a nice, plump ass, calling to be squeezed and fucked.

My cock hardened at the thought of her warm, brown eyes staring into mine. I imagined her full, naked breasts and tiny waist begging to be handled.

"She needs a bit of help," Saph continued. "Rosie's never had an orgasm before, and I know you're attracted to her. I want you to give her an experience she'll never forget, and I want to be a voyeur."

"Saph."

"Please?"

"No."

"Please, Julian! Just this once!"

"Saph, I'm not sure. I don't want to share you with anyone—man or woman."

"I don't need to join in. I'll repeat myself—I want to be a voyeur."

"Sapphire Blake, do you really know what you're talking us into?"

"Julian, please! Do it for me! I want this." I turned my head away and viewed city lights twinkling in the darkness. "C'mon, Julian! You fucked for a living before. You've taught me everything so far, and I want to keep learning from you."

"I'm reluctant to say yes on this one. I've lost you before, and I won't lose you again."

"You won't lose me, Julian. I'm begging you, please!"

I shook my head and sighed.

"This is the only time I'm asking you to do something for me in the bedroom. I won't get jealous, and I'm pansexual—I'm attracted to people for who they are, regardless of their gender identity."

"I know."

"Professor Richland, please!"

I drew in the night air, exhaled, then groaned. "I'll do it once, but never ask me again."

"Okay, I promise." Saph smiled seductively like Aphrodite emerging from the foamy sea.

What had I created out of the sweet Sapphire Blake? The innocent virgin was long gone. Was her mind ever innocent? How easily people can be corrupted, even those with goodness in their hearts. The young nobles who supported the Roman politician Appius in his tyranny were such men, according to Machiavelli. Was I a tyrant, and was Saph my noblewoman? Anxiety was never too far away from us, and hope seemed all the more deceptive.

Chapter Twenty-One
Sapphire's Gift

Julian
Friday night, three weeks later

"I'm telling you, man—if a CEO of a Fortune 500 company went to prison, he'd be at the bottom of the pecking order," Matt exclaimed amid the loud music at Tango, a trendy nightclub in the middle of the city.

I took a swig of my beer, eyeing the crowded bar and the full dance floor. I spotted a group of college girls pointing in my direction, shamelessly smiling and flirting at my buddy and me.

"You can be an alpha in one group, and a beta in another," Matt continued, running his fingers through his blond hair.

"I'm not arguing with that." I chuckled at Matt's theory. "We're all capable of switching between being dominant and submissive, depending on the circumstances."

"Ah, Julian! You and the ladies," Matt said, grinning at the girls, who paraded toward as.

"Professors Richland and Kennedy. We weren't planning on finding two hot college professors here tonight," the alpha of the group announced, stepping toward us. She leaned over, revealing a pair of tanned tits from her gray micro halterneck top, and took a sip of my beer.

"Excuse me, do I know you?" I took the beer back, moving it away from her.

"Sure you do, prof! I'm in your class, and I always get my front-row seat in your lecture theatre," she flirted, while her posse of friends giggled.

"Professor Kennedy, I'm in your class. Oh my gosh, I can't believe you're here tonight," one of the alpha's sidekicks prattled, winking at Matt.

The alpha took another step closer to me, attempting to touch my arm.

"Funny, I don't remember you at all," I said coldly, moving my arm away from her.

"Sure you do, prof. I've been eye-fucking you all semester," she bullshitted.

"What's your name, kid?" I asked.

"Stephanie. Stephanie Milan."

"Stephanie Milan, let me tell you something. Firstly, I recall your name now. If you had spent more time focusing on the content of the lectures instead of eye-fucking, you might have passed the marked paper I'm about to hand out next week."

"What are you saying, prof? Are you saying that I failed?"

"Bingo, sweetheart. Secondly, I can speak freely since I'm not at work right now. You see those doors over there by the entrance?"

"Yeah. What about them?"

"My girlfriend is about to walk through those doors, and you don't want to fuck with her. She's like a Ferrari, a real smooth ride, and when she purrs, she's a fucking fantastic experience. Now, why would I want to trade my baby girl for anything less?"

I leaned back, smirked, and folded my arms in satisfaction.

"Understood, sir." Stephanie's eyes glowered at me while her friends backed away, taking her hand.

"Stephanie?"

"Yes, sir?"

"You can fuck off now."

"Shit, Julian, you've broken the poor girl's heart." Matt grinned, sipped his beer, and watched the college girls walk toward the restroom.

"I broke her pride, not her heart," I corrected him. "How's the missus?"

"She went back to work after Jackson started at daycare a week ago."

"How's that going?"

"It's busy times, man. It's busy times." Matt rubbed his forehead, smiling with satisfaction.

"Cheers, mate. Cheers to life and your family." I raised my beer glass, and he followed suit.

No drink was more refreshing than a glass of ice-cold beer. Matt was busy these days, but it was good to catch up over a few beers now and then.

"Hey, sweetie!" A beautiful woman wearing an emerald satin dress moved toward me. She wore the Cartier bracelet I'd bought her for Christmas a while ago, and her sapphire eyes lit up the room.

Her smile.

Her smile.

Her enigmatic smile.

"Saph!" I exclaimed, breaking from the trance of gazing at my lover's smooth, alabaster face.

"Hey, I'm Matt Kennedy. I work with your boyfriend." Matt got up and shook Saph's hand.

"Nice to meet you, Matt. I'm Sapphire Blake. Julian's told me a bit about you."

"All good things, I hope."

"All good things," she assured him.

"Julian, I've got to run—I don't want to miss the next train, or Tanya won't be pleased." Matt winked, indicating that he planned to get laid that night. "Good to finally meet you, Sapphire. I'm sure we'll catch up again soon," he said, before leaving the nightclub.

I looked at my woman and realized she wasn't alone. Rosie stood behind her, shyly glancing at me. Sapphire had brought me a gift, wrapped in a transparent puff sleeve crop top with leopard prints, and a pair of tight, midnight-black leather pants. Rosie was stunning, and I intended to undress my gift that night.

"Rosie, it's good to see you again." I smiled.

"Likewise," she replied.

Saph walked to my side, massaging my shoulders. "Shall we go back to your place, Julian?" she asked.

"Very well, then." I took her hand, kissed it, then stood up. I pulled her in, pressed her red lips with mine, and whispered, "Now."

***

Thirty minutes later, the three of us gazed at the city view from my apartment balcony. I held Saph tightly, kissing her smooth neck and pressing my groin into her lower back, while she gazed at Rosie. Rosie took two hits of a joint, before passing it to Saph.

"No, thanks. I'll pass." Saph politely declined the joint and gave it to me.

"What's the matter, love?"

"I was feeling a little dizzy earlier today, so I'm not going to test my luck."

I inhaled, taking in a slow breath, and felt the smoke travel down my windpipe, filling my lungs. I gazed at Rosie, took her hand, and brought her closer to me. Her eyes looked down while her body trembled.

"I'm just a little cold," she admitted.

"Let me warm you up, baby," I murmured, breathing in Rosie's coconut scent. "Mmm, you smell good, Rosie." I shifted my body, so Saph leaned on my right side, rubbing my shoulder and kissing my neck, while I caressed Rosie's waist.

"It's Coconut Passion by Victoria's Secret," Rosie revealed.

"It will be the only thing you'll wear later tonight," I assured her, kissing her neck, then her shoulder.

It was close to midnight when we went inside my bedroom. Rosie and I enjoyed the effects of a few drinks and the cannabis. I felt the dopamine kick in, creating a euphoric and relaxed sensation. Saph didn't drink or smoke that evening, but she was a horny little sex kitten on heels. She had already started undressing herself, revealing a red bustier and tiny lace thong.

"Do I get to fuck you tonight, Saph?" I lay on the bed, smiling as I watched her pull up a chair and sit on it, spreading her legs wide open.

"No, sweetie. Tonight it's my rules. I want to watch you and Rosie fuck, and she's not leaving this apartment without an orgasm."

"That's right, Julian," Rosie whispered, climbing on top of me.

I untied the front straps that held Rosie's blouse together, and my cock rose to life when I saw her naked, large breasts. They had to be natural double Ds.

"Hey, look at me." My left finger gently lifted Rosie's face, so I met her eye to eye. "Don't be shy. I don't bite."

She let out a soft chuckle and smiled at me. "Are you sure about that?"

"I'm sure. Well, I don't bite that hard." I threw a devilish smile.

I massaged her soft, ample breasts, sat up, and took each swollen nipple with my lips. Her nipples stiffened when I teased them with my tongue. I shifted my eyes toward Saph, who slowly removed her thong, revealing her shaven sex. She started to finger herself, repetitively dipping two fingers in and out of her bare pussy.

"Look at Rosie, baby. Isn't she pretty?" Saph prompted.

"Your nipples are perfect, like sweet, chocolate gumdrops," I said to Rosie, who unbuttoned my shirt and threw it on the floor.

She undid my belt, unbuckled the buttons of my jeans, and took them off. Her tight pants joined mine a few seconds later. She wore no underwear. I smiled and observed her naked pussy, which featured a thin strip of neatly trimmed pubic hair.

"You're fucking beautiful," I exclaimed, skillfully rubbing her pussy with my fingers.

"Hmm, what do we have here?" She licked her lips, gazing at my tented boxers, before whipping them off.

She gasped in surprise, covering her mouth with both hands. "Saph! He's magnificent!" Rosie's eyes fired up with tantalizing excitement.

"Here, touch me." I encouraged her to stroke my stiff cock, which tilted upward. "You did this, Rosie." I smiled as she continued massaging my manhood.

"Girl, there's no way you're missing this once-in-a-lifetime opportunity," my girlfriend said.

Rosie lowered her head, then began sucking on my cock. Her tongue swirled around the head, licking it like a lollipop.

"Oh, fuck, that feels amazing!" I gasped, stroking her hair. "You have a very talented little mouth, Rosie."

Saph continued playing with herself, moaning at the sight of her friend giving me pleasure. Her delectable breasts seemed rounder and fuller, and her face appeared flushed with sensual satisfaction. She was so fucking sexy; the woman was my lover.

"Look into my eyes as she licks you. Imagine that it's my tongue stroking you up and down your shaft," Miss Blue Eyes commanded. God, who was this rousing siren, beckoning me to her call?

A low groan escaped my lips as Rosie continued sucking on my knob while using her hand to stroke up and down my shaft. Having full control of my cock, she nursed it with her seductive mouth and eager tongue, stimulating its arousal and excitement. I felt a wave of ecstasy rising, but it was too soon. I wanted to taste Rosie first. I gently pulled her head back and whispered to her, "Lie back and relax."

She obeyed my command, and I spread her legs, opening her vaginal lips.

"You're exquisite," I murmured, drawing close to her fleshy sex.

Slowly, I worked one finger into her anal hole as I started to lick her clitoris.

"Oh, sweetness!" Rosie cried, as I sucked on her clit.

"That's it, Julian. Give her what she wants," Saph encouraged.

I continued sucking and teasing Rosie with my tongue for a while, and her cries grew louder. Her body shivered and quaked as my tongue savored her creamy wetness, while my finger explored inside her tight anus. "Your pussy is so tasty, Rosie," I murmured, breathing hotly into her sex.

"Oh, Julian, I want your cock!" she begged, as her fingernails dug into my shoulders.

I stopped, sat up, and looked at Saph, who continued rubbing her clit, moaning as she watched me prepare to give her friend the fuck of her life. She nodded, signaling approval, so I took a condom from the bedside table and rolled it on my dick.

"Come here, baby," Rosie called out, pulling me into her. I aimed my fully erect cock at her, placing it at the entrance of her sex. "Hold me around the waist," she beckoned, as I shoved my cock inside her. She was wet and slippery, and her cream encircled the base of my cock.

"Damn, Julian! You're pure magic!" Rosie gushed under her breath, parting her thighs even more.

I chuckled and caressed her ass cheek with one hand, melding her body deeper into mine. "You like this, don't you?" I asked, matching Rosie thrust for thrust as her hips bucked into mine.

"I love what you're doing to me, and I've never felt this way. Julian, do you want me?" Rosie moaned, rocking her body with mine as my cock continued thrusting in and out of her.

"Answer her question," Saph ordered.

"I want you, Rosie. You turn me on," my voice rasped deeply, drugged by the sex. I drove my cock further in, moving together with her steadily at first, then at a quicker pace to escalate the waves of pleasure. I peered at Saph, who panted with desire and finger fucked her wet, swollen clit while watching me have sex with another woman. My heart ached for my angel, wanting her to join me.

Intoxicated with the drugging effect of pre-orgasmic tremors, tears of pleasure trickled down Rosie's flushed cheeks as we fucked each other with excitement. "Fill me, Julian! I want you now," Rosie pleaded, holding my body tightly.

I rammed into her, not holding back, and increased the speed of my thrusts. I kissed her mouth, and my tongue mimicked our sex, plunging and thrashing until she came, crying out in pleasure and arching her back in stillness, before breaking into involuntary quivers.

I joined her, shuddering as I ejaculated. I cried out as my enjoyment climaxed, overtaking my body. I looked over to Sapphire, who shook and cried as she hit an orgasmic high, letting out her release. Then it hit me—I had imagined being in Saph when I came inside Rosie. I couldn't do this shit anymore. I removed the used condom, tied it, and threw it in a wastebasket near the bed. A moment later, I rested on the bed with Rosie on my left and Saph on my right before falling into a deep sleep.

Sapphire
Saturday morning

Rosie, Julian, and I enjoyed a warm shower together, but Rosie declined breakfast, saying that she had to work at the café soon and would grab some food on the go.

Rosie thanked us for the evening before she left the apartment. "I'll never forget this," she said, grinning from ear to ear.

Julian, bless his kind heart, had bought me gluten-free cornflakes for breakfast and stocked his fridge and cupboard with food that I could eat. He made room for me in his apartment—the wardrobe in the guest room started to fill with spare clothes and toiletries that I brought along with me.

After breakfast with Julian, I was relaxing on his leather sofa, reading his copy of Machiavelli's *The Prince*, when a warm hand snaked down my décolletage, lifting the cloth of my blouse. The hand touched my naked skin, massaged my right breast, and toyed with my nipple.

"Julian! You caught me by surprise." I turned and looked at him.

The man was the epitome of dark, brooding sexiness, even in a simple Levis t-shirt and a pair of jeans. His left arm displayed a sports watch and a black leather band. His hair was uncombed, indicating a hint of his chilled mood that followed a night of hot sex.

"I'm just going to clean up a little. You can stay as long as you like," he said.

"Do you need any help?" I offered, placing the book face down on the coffee table.

"Nah, I'll be fine. The cleaner is coming in a few days."

I picked up the book and continued reading, then saw Julian walk out of the bedroom with last night's pillowcase covers and bedsheets, heading toward the laundry room.

"Julian's a neat freak," Vera had said to me once.

He then returned to the bedroom, where I heard some shuffling, followed by the loud sound of the vacuum whirring. After a while, I stepped into the room and watched him vacuuming every corner around the bed, which had new sheets and pillowcases.

"Are you sure you don't need help?"

"Huh?" Julian stopped the vacuum and looked up.

"Are you sure you don't need help?" I repeated.

"You can open the windows to let in some fresh air," he suggested.

He placed scented incense sticks on his bedside table, and the fragrance of sweet chai and lavender slowly penetrated the cool, freshened air.

After fifteen minutes of helping Julian with meticulous cleaning, I returned to the sofa and continued reading. Julian walked toward his keyboard, sat down, and started playing "My Girl" by The Temptations. He began to sing as he played, which completely caught me by surprise. It was a song Cameron once sang to me when things were sweet with him, but that was the past. I had a new man in my life singing the same song, and his voice was just as beautiful.

"Julian, I had no idea you could sing so well," I exclaimed when he finished his song.

"You never asked," he replied, playing a little melody on the piano.

He then stopped playing and turned to me. "Saph, I'm tired. The thing is, I don't think I can do this." His dark eyes were troubled.

My heart dropped. "What do you mean, you can't do this?" I demanded.

"I'm not a piece of meat, Saph. I'm tired of being everyone's lover."

"Julian—"

"The truth is, this love is new for me. I've never felt this way for another woman—just you. Saph, I love you very much. My feelings are intense, and I have this strong compulsion to make you mine, and mine only."

"What about you, Julian? Are you mine too?"

"Saph—"

"Well? Are you? If we jump into a serious relationship, we can be open, or we can be closed. However, I won't accept double standards. It won't work for me."

"It has to work for you. I won't share you, and you don't want double standards. So, there's one option left. Let's close the door to every temptation that knocks."

"It's a big step for us, Julian."

"It is: It's called a commitment, sweetheart. I'm selfish, but not without reason. I want a closed relationship. I want you exclusively to myself, and I want to offer you the same."

His espresso eyes bathed in a whirlpool of dark, ravenous hunger and sparkled with joy. Pure. Genuine. Joy.

Chapter Twenty-Two
Julian's Gift

Sapphire
One week later

"Raphael, a reporter from the *Lester Harbor City News* wants to interview Paul at two o'clock next Tuesday."

"It's not doable. His calendar is booked for the day."

"If you move the weekly team meeting to three-thirty, he'll have time for the phone interview. It's a positive news piece about his vision for the economy in this neck of the woods."

"Nope." Raphael's blank stare and folded arms indicated hostility, which had lingered in the air since the night of the university dinner.

"Don't be a stubborn idiot," I replied. "You manage his work calendar, so move the bloody meeting, or I'll walk into Paul's office and tell him myself."

Another dizzy spell just hit me, and I felt the nausea creep from my gut to my throat.

"Are you sick, Saph? You look pale."

"No, I'm not well. I'll be back."

A few minutes later, I flushed away the remains of my lunch that I'd vomited into the toilet. I broke into a sweat and tried to control my nausea with some breathing techniques I'd learned from yoga class. This was more than food poisoning. My breasts were fuller, and my bloodhound nose was more sensitive to the smells around me. I walked out of the bathroom after washing my hands and returned to my desk.

"Are you alright, Saph? You should go home if you're sick. Whatever virus you've got, I don't want to share it with you," Raphael said.

Idiot. You can't catch this type of germ from me, Raphael.

"I'm going home."

"Good idea."

"Raphael, do me a favor. Change next Tuesday's team meeting to three-thirty and confirm the two o'clock slot with the journo from the *City News*."

Raphael gave me a smile out of pity and nodded his head.

I arrived home after a quick stop at the pharmacy, where I bought a pregnancy test kit. *Oh boy. Here goes nothing.* I pulled out my cell phone from my handbag and called the closest friend I had—Vera. I needed her more than ever, as my emotions were running high.

"Saph, what's up?"

"Vera, can you come over straight after work?"

"Are you crying, hon?"

"It doesn't matter if I'm crying. I need your help."

"Aww, hon! Of course. Are you at home right now?"

"Yes."

"I can finish my day early and come over in the next half hour or so."

"Thanks."

Thirty minutes later

"Honey, what's going on?"

I had just let Vera into my apartment, and she'd already noticed my puffy eyes. I just shook my head in response.

"Is it my brother?"

I nodded as the tears streamed down my face.

"Vera, I missed my last period, and my next one is due now. The thing is, I don't think it'll come for a long while."

"Oh my!" Vera's eyes grew wide and round. "Have you taken a test yet?"

"Not yet, but I've got one in the bathroom."

"Go take the test right now, girl!"

Three minutes later

Oh. My. God. The pregnancy test stick showed a plus sign. Shit. Julian and I had had wild, rough, and mind-blowing unprotected sex on the night of the university dinner, and now I was paying for it. I came out of the bathroom with the used pregnancy test stick in my hand and revealed the result to Vera.

"Oh, Vera! I should never have gone off the pill a few months back," I moaned.

She clicked her tongue and shook her head, shifting her position on the sofa. "Welp! You've really done it. You and my brother. Congrats," she stated, with a hint of sarcasm.

"Vera, this is serious! If I keep the baby, this is going to change my life! Either way, I have to tell Julian."

"Yep. It takes two to do the horizontal tango, and you're both in it together."

"We were so stupid not to use protection! I thought my period was around the corner, and Julian assured me he was clean."

"Yeah, that was pretty stupid. You just don't take risks. But then again, Saph, I learned one thing about you—you like playing with fire when it comes to Jules."

Vera chuckled as I groaned.

"I thought it was safe enough if my period stuck to its schedule."

"Oh, honey! You can't trust your cycle, especially if you've been irregular due to stress. Seriously, Saph? You know this!"

Vera may as well have skewered me with her astute stare. She made a great lawyer, and she knew it.

"You can be honest. A part of you probably wanted this, am I right?"

I nodded my head.

"So, when will you tell him?"

"Soon. He's out with some friends from work this evening, so I don't want to dampen his night. Do you think Julian will flip?"

"Nah."

"Really? I mean, this will change his life. I'm considering the other option—an abortion. I mean, it's not exactly planned."

Vera lifted her left eyebrow and pursed her lips tightly. I forgot that she and Julian were Roman Catholics and didn't believe in abortion as the first resort to solving such self-inflicted problems—in my case.

"He's going to freak out." I buried my face in my hands.

"Nope."

"Huh?"

"Think about it. He's extremely neat, he's meticulous, and he's OCD when it comes to details."

"What are you saying, Vera?"

"I've never known Julian to be sloppy. His high school and college assignments were flawless. Everything he did was with care."

"I know. You were right about him being a neat freak." I let out a weak smile.

"Jules takes the greatest care not to knock anyone up or catch any diseases. He gets regular health checks, you know, and he loves you so much he wouldn't dream of putting you at risk," Vera said.

"Yeah, except for being tested positive for pregnancy." I rolled my eyes and sighed. Another wave of nausea rose again.

"My point exactly."

"You think he planned to put a baby in me?"

"What do you think?"

"Fuck! Fucking shit."

"No shit, Sherlock!" Vera snorted in her laughter. "I've got to admit, I've never seen my brother become so intensely involved with anyone before. Well, there's a first time for everything."

My eyebrows shot up at her comment, remembering that Julian had taken my virginity too.

"Oh, sorry, no pun intended!" Vera yelped.

That girl and I were riding on the same wavelength, and I laughed with her. I remembered Lady Hope telling me there was no point crying over spilled milk, so I preferred to laugh instead.

"I'm so glad that you're turning that frown upside down, Saph. If you decide to keep the baby, your story isn't over. You've got a great life ahead of you," Vera encouraged.

"Well, what's the point of crying when what's done is done?" I pondered loudly.

"He's a great guy, Saph," Vera assured. "You need to keep an open mind when it comes to Julian, but give him a chance, and I promise he will give you more than you ask for."

"Oh, he's already given me more than I asked for," I joked, patting my still flat belly.

"On another note, if you want to keep the baby, I'm looking forward to being an aunt!" Vera beamed with enthusiasm.

***

I stared at the bathroom mirror during my lunch break at work the next day, and I wondered how my life would be in less than nine months.

I tried to hold back my tears, because I wasn't sure if I was ready to be a mother, let alone be the mother of Julian's child.

Let it out, sweetie. Wicked Anxiety gently massaged my stressed shoulders.

"I shouldn't be crying over spilled milk." I sighed loudly.

Hope is full of shit. Sometimes you need to let it out, sis. Let it out. Wicked Anxiety folder her arms.

The tears spilled...

One tear.

Two tears.

More tears.

One by one.

You're anxious. There's a life growing in you and not much promise from that man of yours. I don't see a ring or a house with a white picket fence.

"I'm worried about the future," I admitted.

You have every reason to be worried. After you tell him about the baby, don't expect a ring. Julian doesn't believe in marriages of convenience. Wicked Anxiety's long, sharp nails started to claw my skin.

How dare you steal her hope? Lady Hope hollered, pushing Wicked Anxiety away.

Hope? False hope in this institution called marriage was the reason this girl's mother married her father. Wicked Anxiety stood tall, refusing to budge.

My parents' wedding date was six months before I was born.

Sapphire, your mother's belief in me gave you a family! Lady Hope's voice boomed.

It's a farce of a family. David never loved Sylvia! Wicked Anxiety shouted back, glaring at Lady Hope.

I knew Wicked Anxiety told the truth. Hope and honesty didn't always go hand in hand.

Have hope, Saph. You and Julian are not your parents. Lady Hope walked away, leaving me alone to deal with my anxiety.

I ran into Raphael in the hallway after walking out of the bathroom a few minutes later.

"Saph, what's going on? If you're sick, you should take another day off work."

"Raphael, it's fine."

"No, it's not fine. No matter what happened between us, I still care about you." His hazel eyes met mine with warmth.

"Raphael, I'm pregnant."

"Holy fuck! It's not mine, is it? We always used condoms, so it can't be mine."

"No, Raphael. It's Julian's. I missed my period last month."

Raphael smirked and ran his hands through his hair in relief. "Listen, you need to talk to Paul, so he knows why you're not feeling well," he suggested. "If he gives you trouble, let me know, and I'll deal with him."

"Raphael, thank you so much."

"Have you told Julian yet?"

"I tried to call him all morning, but my calls went straight to voicemail."

"Good luck with that. If you need a shoulder to cry on, I'm here."

I nodded, and Raphael gave me a firm pat on my shoulders.

Later that day

"Hello?"

"Saph, you tried to call."

"Yeah, I missed you earlier today."

"Sorry, love. I was busy teaching classes. How is my sweetheart?"

"I'm okay. Julian, would you have time to meet this week?"

"Always. I always have time for you. How about my place tomorrow evening? Six o'clock? I'll cook you dinner."

"I'll see you then, Julian."

"Saph?"

"Yes, darling?"

"I love you."

"I love you too, Julian. I'll see you tomorrow."

Chapter Twenty-Three
Renewed Hope

Sapphire

"Darling, can you stir the pot while I grab some wine?" Julian directed his gaze at me, while his elbow gently nudged mine. He was alluring, even when he wore a simple, gray V-neck t-shirt and an old pair of jeans.

Honestly, the guy didn't need to wear much to look so goddamn sexy. I admired the way he moved in the kitchen—from when he chopped and prepared the vegetables, to when he cooked the chicken pieces with crushed garlic cloves, olive oil, bay leaves, and rosemary sprigs. Unfortunately, my stomach churned when I breathed in the garlic-infused meal, and the thought of wine was enough for the powerfully acidic bile to rise in my throat.

"Honey, I'm not drinking any wine tonight," I replied.

"Not even a glass?"

Julian wrapped his left arm around me and planted a warm kiss on my lips while the dulcet tones of "Unchained Melody" by the Righteous Brothers played in the background.

"No, darling."

"Saph? Is everything alright?" His mysterious eyes held mine captive with concern.

I placed my hands on his torso and gently rubbed his body, gazing into his eyes with an aching need.

"Julian, I think the chicken cacciatore is done."

He turned off the stove and placed a lid over the pot, before taking my hand and leading me to the sofa.

"Sit down, love. You don't look so well."

We sat, facing each other, on his leather sofa while his hands encapsulated mine, stroking them gently. I couldn't hold it anymore and let the tears spill uncontrollably. I blamed it on the fucking pregnancy hormones, which were causing my moods to swing faster than the pendulum of a grandfather clock. My HCG levels must have skyrocketed in the past twenty-four hours.

"Saph, is there something you want to tell me?"

"Julian, I'm so sorry."

Julian's face froze with a combination of fear and anxiety.

"What did you do?"

"It's not what I did alone. It's what we did together."

"Saph? Stop talking in riddles and say it to me straight. I'm a grown man, not some college kid."

"Julian, do you remember the night of the university dinner and the Sunday afterward? To put it bluntly, I'm pregnant with your child as a result."

"Wait, love? You're carrying my child?" Julian's eyes blinked with surprise, and his eyebrows shot up.

"Yes, I'm pregnant. Are you okay, Julian?"

"I'm more than okay. I'm going to be a father!" Julian's mouth opened wide, forming a joyous smile that was filled to the brim with excitement.

"I'm going to be a mother." I felt an air of hope filter through the living room, bringing relief and happiness.

"Darling, you're everything I want in a woman—a lover, and as my future wife and mother of my child," he declared, revealing his straight, white teeth through a generous grin.

My heart swelled with hope as I leaned forward and rested my head on the wide breadth of his shoulder. While the smell of the garlic meal—which would have tasted divine under normal circumstances—made my stomach churn, Julian's aroma had the opposite effect. The scent of his fresh, citrus body wash combined with his natural pheromones assailed my nostrils, so I breathed him in with comforting delight. My lover's scent had a way of easing my nausea, and I couldn't imagine being with another soul. I suddenly had hope that our pregnancy would bring us closer than ever.

Julian pressed his lips against mine, rewarding me with a deep kiss while probing my tongue with his hunger.

"Saph?" He breathed heavily, and his bedroom eyes grew darker.

"Yes, darling," I murmured.

Our heads touched while our hands played with each other.

"I love you, Saph." Julian's eyes lowered, showing off his long, dark lashes. "I feel a strong urge to protect you, to hold you, and to make sure you never lack any form of love—neither you nor my child."

"What do you want, Julian?"

"I want you to move in with me. Live with me. Let me give you everything your heart desires. I want to be that man for you, the man who gives you the world you want."

A piece of his mahogany hair fell onto his forehead, and my fingers itched to touch it. I brushed it aside, then ran my fingers through his hair, bringing him closer to me.

"Yes. I will move in with you, Julian. I love you," I whispered, before drugging him with a kiss from my lips, sealing the deal.

"Saph?" Julian broke the kiss with one more question. "I want to ask you to marry me one day. Would you like this to happen before or after the baby is born?"

"After the baby is born. Right now, we've got a full plate adjusting to parenthood," I replied.

"We sure do things a little unconventionally," Julian chuckled.

"Not really. More and more people are living together before they marry. It's quite common these days," I refuted. I knew I was right.

"Ah, there's a conservative Catholic boy inside me wanting to do things a little more traditionally, love."

It was my turn to chuckle now. "Says the wicked Julian Richland to the conservative Sapphire Blake," I teased.

"You, my love, have no idea what you're talking about." Julian tickled the side of my rib cage, eliciting a bubble of laughter from me.

"STOP! Stop it, Julian!" I begged for mercy between the giggles.

"We'll tell our families the good news. Mom will be thrilled, and I'm sure Vera will be pleased to have a little niece or nephew."

"Uhm, about that ... Vera was there when I took the pregnancy test."

"Oh! Why am I not surprised? My little sister has always enjoyed meddling with my life." Julian shrugged his shoulders and feigned surrender.

"I'm looking forward to sharing the news with your family," I exclaimed.

"Our family, love. They're your family now."

My heart rose, then fell at the thought of my own family.

"I wish I could say the same about my parents," I admitted.

"One day, love. We'll take each day as it comes," Julian assured me.

I kissed his unshaven jaw, then worked down the nape of his neck, while sliding my hands under his shirt to feel his muscled body. It was only a matter of minutes before we were both naked, kissing, and exploring each other's bodies. I lay on the sofa, arching beneath him as his manly chest pressed against the fullness of my breasts.

"We're in this together, Saph," he murmured, feeling my bare belly with his strong hands.

His gaze raked over me, and his eyes were clouded with desire.

"I love you endlessly, Julian," I whispered as my fingers played in circular motions with the dark hairs that curled around the nape of his neck.

"This is mine," he growled, feeling where his child was growing.

"Yours," I affirmed.

"I love seeing you naked. I want to see you every day, especially as your body changes."

His cock prodded at my wet entrance, and its head teased by dipping in and out, creating heated excitement. Each time he dipped in, he went a little deeper, causing me to ache for him more.

"Oh, Julian!" I moaned. Inflamed with playful seduction, I wrapped my legs around his hips, rocking my pelvis and savoring the sensation of his sex, which made a full, grand invasion.

I rubbed against my lover as he filled me with his hard, thick penis, rendering me intoxicated with delicious desire. With every movement of my hips, I allowed more of him to enter me, while he kissed me, filling my mouth with his tongue. He continued thrusting in me, jerking his hips against mine, until I felt I was about to tip over the edge with a drugged effect of orgasmic tremors. I cried out in sheer pleasure, feeling my body quiver in ecstasy as he stiffened, shouted my name, and shook from his orgasmic ejaculation.

A moment later, we snuggled into each other and tried to catch our breaths. He stroked my hair repetitively, kissing my forehead with gentle passion.

"My heart belongs to you," he whispered, before we drifted into heavy sleep.

***

About an hour later, I woke up feeling very sick.

"Julian, I need something to eat and drink. Fast!" I tapped the arm of my sleeping lover.

His eyes slowly opened, registering that I needed his help.

"Honey?" His lashes fluttered as he got up and put on his boxer shorts.

"I need something salty and dry, and a fizzy drink to help with my unsettled stomach," I said.

"Go and rest in my bed. I'll come to you with some food," he promised.

I found my panties on the floor, wriggled into them, then headed toward his room to grab one of his old shirts. However, my stomach couldn't hold itself, so I ran into the bathroom, opened the toilet lid, and vomited water and the snacks that I'd eaten earlier that afternoon. A moment later, Julian lifted me from the tiled bathroom floor and helped me wash my face at the sink.

"Here, brush your teeth, darling. You'll feel better." He handed me my toothbrush, and I placed some toothpaste on the bristles. Even the minty taste of the toothpaste was slightly off when I tasted it.

A few minutes after, I lay in bed with a plate of crackers on the bedside table. Julian handed me a glass of tonic water.

"I'm so sorry you have to go through this, darling," he sighed, as I took small sips of the fizzy water.

"Here, try these rice crackers. The salt will help ease the pain," he coaxed. I slowly nibbled the wheat-free crackers, glancing at him.

"You need to eat more, love." His dark eyes expressed genuine concern.

"Julian, I can't. This is all I can manage right now," I cried.

"So, I guess that's a 'no' to chicken cacciatore tonight?" Julian released a small, lopsided grin.

I shook my head with intense fervor.

"Well, I'll put it away in the fridge. If you change your mind, let me know."

"Julian, I can't take garlic right now," I sighed, rubbing my temples.

"Roger that."

"This isn't going to be easy, is it? It wasn't entirely planned—I mean, the way I wanted my life to be."

"Unplanned doesn't necessarily mean unwanted or unloved. I don't think it will be easy, but it will be worth it." Julian placed his left hand on my belly, delivering an assurance of hope. "I'll be your family, and I'll give you the house with a white picket fence," he said.

"Will you still love me when things get ugly, like what you saw this evening?" I asked.

"Saph, I'm not shallow and vain."

"I know. It's just these bloody hormones that are making me emotional. I love you so much, Julian."

"*Sapphire*, I love you, endlessly. You are my family now."

Chapter Twenty-Four
Baby Love

Sapphire
Saturday, September 9

"What do you think, love?" Julian was grinning from ear to ear, staring at our new home.

"It's beautiful, Julian. I love it!" I smiled, rubbing my pregnant belly, which was in full bloom.

I was at the end of my second trimester, and the severe morning sickness was long gone. I'd suffered from hyperemesis gravidarum (HG) in my first trimester, and Julian had taken me to the hospital several times for IV treatments. I experienced severe nausea, vomiting, weight loss, and dehydration, all symptoms of HG. I lost about ten pounds but put it back on at the start of my second trimester, thanks to my doctor, who prescribed an anti-nausea medication for me.

The second trimester was a much better experience for my man and me. Our sex life was back on track; in fact, I was hungrier than ever for Julian's cock. We both blamed it on my crazy pregnancy hormones. My doctor confirmed that sex was safe with my partner during the pregnancy, and it would not hurt the baby.

"This house is gorgeous, Julian," I assured him, rubbing his solid arm.

We stood in front of an enviable three-bedroom brick home with a white picket fence and a lush, green garden. We'd picked a house in a quiet neighborhood close to where Julian's mom, Frances, lived. We'd rented out the apartment to a young couple who worked in the city, as it was an investment that would provide long-term returns for us.

"I'm glad you're happy with our new home, because we're not getting a refund." Julian gently poked my rib with his elbow, eliciting laughter from my lips.

"I can just picture our son learning to walk in this garden," I said.

Julian and I had discovered from our last ultrasound result that we were having a baby boy, who was growing at a healthy rate. The child's health was important to me.

"This is our home from here on," Julian murmured, kissing my neck, as he held me in a tight embrace.

The inside of the house was just as gorgeous as the exterior—it was adorned with polished timber floors, grand windows to let in the natural sunlight, and an open-plan kitchen with contrasting stone countertops. All the bedrooms had walk-in wardrobes, air conditioning for the hot summers, and good heating for the cold winter months.

"This is a dream," I praised, turning to my partner.

I suddenly felt a series of kicks, then took Julian's hand to touch his active child, who continued moving in my womb.

"It's amazing what you're growing in there, Saph," he said, looking directly into my eyes. "The good thing about living here is that Mom's place is just a stone's throw away. You can even walk there." He folded his arms and looked out the window.

"I probably will. The furniture transport company's truck should be here any minute now." I looked down at my watch, which was set a few minutes faster than the actual time.

"Mom and Vera will be here soon to help us unpack. It's in their best interest that you shouldn't be lifting anything too heavy."

I sighed, thinking of my own family. In contrast to Frances's tears of joy when we'd told her about the pregnancy, my mother had cried tears of disappointment.

"You have put shame to this family, Sapphire! My daughter is an unwed mother who carries a playboy's bastard child! Do you honestly believe that man will stick around?" Mom wailed on the phone. "Your father refuses to acknowledge you, and for the first time in my life, I am truly ashamed of you!" Those were my mother's words before she hung up on me.

Julian said that it was their loss, and they would miss out on the real joys of family in the future.

He was right.

4:00 p.m.

"Are you hungry?" Vera asked, eyeing my baby bump.

Cardboard boxes surrounded us in the baby's room.

"Contrary to popular belief, I feel less hungry as the baby takes up more space. I swear, it's like an alien invasion happening inside me," I stated, shaking my head.

"I can see a little smile under that frown," Vera teased.

"I'm sure Julian and your mom are hungry, so go ahead and order pizza. There's a local gourmet pizza company that delivers within the hour. They have gluten-free options for me too," I suggested.

"Sure thing, sweetie." Vera grinned, then got up from the floor.

"JULES! Are you hungry?" she hollered from the corridor, looking down the stairs.

I heard a shuffling of boxes before a delayed response came from downstairs.

"Yes!"

"Do you want pizza?" Vera bellowed.

"Yes!"

"How about Mom?"

"Go ahead and order some pizza, sweetie!" Frances's voice resonated.

"I love your family," I confessed to Vera, when she returned to the room after ordering pizza.

She sat on the floor next to me, crossing her legs. "Growing up with Julian was no walk in the park. He was a pain in the ass sometimes," she chuckled. "He used to scare off my love interests when I was in high school."

"Really?" I looked up at her.

"Yeah. One time, Jules told my date, Andy, that he and his friends would find where the guy lived and make his nights hell if he didn't bring me home from the movies by ten o'clock."

"Wow, that's a protective big brother!"

"Exactly! That was the first and last date I ever went on with Andy. He was a hottie too!"

"Well, if you were still with Andy, we wouldn't have had the fun we enjoyed together," I teased, reminding Vera of the good old days before Julian.

"Yeah, that was until Jules interfered again!" Vera's infectious laugh burst into the room, causing me to break into fits of giggles with her.

A minute later, we had tears of mirth in our eyes, reminiscing about Julian, including the hot shower story, which I finally admitted to her.

"Oh man, I cannot believe you did that while I was buying wheat-free snacks for you!" Vera snickered.

"Well, look where chasing Julian got me." I pointed downward at my round belly, which slightly moved as the baby wriggled in my womb.

"All knocked up!"

We broke out in hives of laughter, only to be interrupted by a tall, sexy man leaning against the door frame. His left leg lazily crossed over the other, and his arms were folded close to his broad chest.

"Vee, are you making fun of me?"

"Jules, I hate being called that!"

"Oh, really?" His left eyebrow arched. "Vee?"

They stared at each other with the same brown eyes. Neither sibling would give up on challenging each other, no matter how big or small the challenge was. Sibling rivalry never died with these two, who were equally smart and stubborn.

"The pizza should be coming soon," I interrupted, breaking the intensity of their stares.

"Good! I'm famished after all this hard work," Vera sighed. "I'm hogging the pepperoni. Julian, you can have the ham and pineapple."

"Are you happy where the piano is?" I glanced at Julian.

"Yeah. I'll play a few songs later."

His eyes begged Vera to give us some privacy—just Julian and me. She took the hint, got up, and shuffled out of the room.

"You two! I always hated being the third wheel." She grinned, patting my arm.

After Vera left the room to join Frances downstairs, Julian fished out two chains with keys from his pocket.

"Saph," he started.

"Oh my! These are gorgeous, Julian!" I gasped, eyeing the antique keys, which rested in his hand.

"These belonged to my father." He glanced down at the keys. "He gave them to my mother, and she wants to pass them to us." He placed one chain around my neck, then put the other around his. "Possessing a key gives a person access to locked rooms," he explained. "In this case, you have the key to my heart, Saph. You have power over me."

I looked into Julian's eyes and saw pure, raw honesty at its finest.

"The key is also a symbol of freedom and liberation," I added. "You love me in such a way that I feel so free."

He started devouring the nape of my neck with hungry kisses. Never in my life had I experienced the intensity of this kind of love before. When I thought of my own family and previous boyfriend, I probably never really had an unconditional and honest love with someone I could trust.

"When my mother and sister are out of the house, I want to christen every room with you," Julian growled, embracing me tightly.

I breathed in his shower-fresh scent, which blended with the natural aroma of a man who'd done a light workout—I exhaled and inhaled his scent again.

"Julian Richland, I love you freely."

"Saph, there is no one who can ever replace you."

Chapter Twenty-Five
Return of the Witch

Sapphire
Sunday, November 5

"Are you nervous?" Julian held my hand.

"A little." I smiled, absorbing the familiar atmosphere of Northern Lakes Baptist Church.

With the baby due in a little over a month, Julian had suggested that we should try to patch things up with my family. So, here we were at a Sunday service, hoping to speak to my mother and father after the sermon.

Pastor Lewis was on fire about diversity in the church during the service.

"Now, I'll tell you a little secret about God. The big man upstairs loves variety. Look around you in this congregation. Look around you when you're at the bus stop, the subway, at work, at school, and in college. We should be celebrating diversity with God! He's no fan of boring sameness, so a deviation from this 'sameness' is both energizing and invigorating! Now, Jesus made friends with people from all walks of life. Let us rejoice!" He lifted his hands in praise, and most of the congregation clapped, including Julian.

However, my father, who was now a stranger to me, sat on the front pew, shaking his head. My mother nodded and smiled in an unnatural, robotic manner. Roland, who had started college, was nowhere in sight.

Cameron, Charlene, and a few former school friends greeted Julian and me in the busy foyer after the service.

"Heya! Wow, you're expecting," Cameron exclaimed, while Charlene eyed my ringless finger.

"So, what happened to your wedding ring? Did you lose it?" Charlene interrogated.

I glowered ruthlessly at Charlene, silently warning her that she was walking on thin ice.

"Yeah, what happened to your ring? When did you get married? Oh, how exciting," Lavinia, who was in my high school math class, gushed. "When's the baby—"

"We're not married yet," I interrupted, disrupting Lavinia's blabber.

Cameron and Charlene's eyes were heavy with judgment.

"Charlene, would you care to cast the first stone?" Julian's sharp words pierced the woman, who blushed and cowered in shame for the prejudice she projected.

I noticed Charlene's third finger on her left hand featured a solitaire diamond ring.

"Congratulations on your engagement, Charlene." I smiled politely, knowing that Julian had given me the upper hand in the conversation.

"Thank you," she replied.

"We're getting married next summer," Cameron proudly announced. "We would love to have you at the wedding."

"Of course we'll be there." I gave a genuine smile while Julian signaled a slight nod.

"It's great to see you both." Pastor Lewis' voice boomed from behind us.

"I see you've got some good news—congratulations!" He shook our hands. "When is the baby due?"

"We're due on December ten," I replied, gently patting my expanding baby bump.

"It's exciting times! I'm happy for you both. Take care." Pastor Lewis clapped my shoulder, shook Julian's hand again, and walked to the next couple.

"It looks like the person of authority enjoys the diversity," I commented.

Julian glanced at Pastor Lewis, who laughed and smiled, not giving a fuck about what the world thought of him.

"I like the guy. He practices what he preaches," Julian said.

Ten minutes later, we approached my mother and father outside the church building as people started to leave. My father's eyes froze on my swollen belly, while my mother covered her mouth, gasping in bewilderment.

"David. Sylvia. Sapphire has something to say." Julian placed one arm around my waist.

"I don't know you." My father's steel-blue eyes stared intensely at me with icy apathy.

"Dad ..." Tears started to run down my cheeks.

Dad's face was stone cold. "I warned you about him, Sapphire. I knew what he was before he met you."

"You ruined Sapphire! She is not my daughter anymore." My mother sneered at Julian, then turned away from us. "Come on, David. Let's go home." She placed her hand on my father's arm, and they walked toward the car park.

"Let it go, love." Julian stroked my hair as I turned to him and wept tears of sorrow on his chest.

"We tried the best we could," I whispered, while Julian's arms kept my body warm.

"Sapphire, they are self-absorbed people who never deserved such a wonderful daughter. It's their loss." He sighed and kissed my forehead.

Saturday, November 11

"Hey, I was next in the queue!"

I tapped the shoulder of a woman who'd stepped in front of me in the line toward the cashier's counter at Pages bookstore.

"I'll take this one." The tall woman pushed her book across the counter, ignoring my statement.

"Excuse me—" I started to speak, then stopped when I realized who it was.

Saira Quinn. The wicked witch of Lester Harbor. My skin crawled, and my stomach flipped with sickness. I felt the baby move, responding to my reaction. I placed my book on the side of the counter, deciding that I would rather leave it there and walk out of the store.

"Oh, Sapphire, was it? What a coincidence!" The ash-blonde snow queen feigned surprise.

I glanced at a paperback copy of *The Portable Machiavelli* on the counter, which Saira paid for with her credit card.

"Oh, it's a good book," she pointed out. "Here, I would like you to have it."

My hands trembled as she handed the book to me.

"Julian has it on his bookshelf," I remarked, giving it back to her.

"I know. Julian knows this book quite well because I gave him my copy."

Saira's eyes focused on my baby bump.

"Dear, you look pale. You remind me of myself when I was pregnant with my son, Damian. How is the pregnancy treating you, Sapphire?"

"That's none of your business, Saira."

"Oh, but it is. I saw on your online CV that you majored in political science in college. You are a clever girl, so I naturally thought of you for an upcoming position as a senior advisor for my dear friend, Senator Colson."

Senator Brian Colson was a member of the opposing political party that lobbied against Paul McGrath. I wasn't about to betray the man who helped me pay my bills.

"Saira, that's very generous of you, but I cannot accept anything right now," I replied.

"Really?" Saira frowned, twitching her mouth to one side. "There are many perks that come with a high-paying job like this one. Think about it. You get to fast-track your career."

"Saira, I don't think so." I shifted my eyes uneasily.

"There are some particularities about this job if you do consider it. It is a great career move, so I would advise that now would not be a wise time to be pregnant," Saira insisted.

She leaned her head to one side and moved closer to me. "It's never too late to terminate the fetus. If you are carrying Julian's child, I'm sure he wouldn't mind. He never wanted children."

"You are fucking crazy!" I snapped in bewilderment.

"Fine. Suit yourself. If you do change your mind, you know where to find me. Here's my card."

I looked at the card and saw it for what it was—a piece of paper and nothing more.

"YOU'RE INSANE!" I shouted, bumping my shoulder against hers as I stormed out of the bookstore. My hatred for Saira was an infernal fury that burned intensely in my soul.

"Sapphire, don't forget your book," the devil called out.

A few minutes later, Wicked Anxiety patted my shoulder as I spewed the contents of my last meal on the ground behind the nearest bus stop.

Ignore the noise, Saph. I'll have fun with her later. The entity gazed at the bookstore, grinning from ear to ear after discovering her newest victim.

"Thank you," I muttered, catching my breath. "Thank you for being here with me."

Julian
Monday, November 13

"Julian, dear, it's good to see you," Saira announced, as I walked into her office.

"I do apologize for keeping you waiting. I'm a busy woman, you see. I have fifteen minutes to spare before I have an appointment with a client. Unless, of course, you have something to offer me. In that case, my client can wait."

"I won't be long; I assure you that," I replied. "I've got one thing to say. Keep away from Sapphire. I don't want you to look at her or speak to her again."

"Whatever do you mean, Julian? I don't understand." Saira's gray eyes bluffed innocence.

"Stop playing games with me. You and I are over, Saira."

"Oh, we are never over, Julian. You and I will always have unfinished matters."

Saira slowly unbuttoned her silk blouse, revealing a pair of perfectly plastic tits. My cock stirred at the heavenly sight, but logic reminded me that this woman was from hell.

Focus, Julian. Focus.

"Put your top back on, Saira. I need you to keep the fuck away from my family."

"Family? Oh, yes, I must congratulate you. Or, should I commiserate with you on your loss of freedom? Women like Sapphire don't take these chances with a blind eye. She's a cunning girl."

"It was my choice. I gave her a child." I averted my eyes from the topless snake, who circled her way around me.

"Oh? What a pity. You and I could have had a great life together."

"Put your bloody top on, woman!" I stepped away from the snake.

"Fine." She covered her naked chest with the blouse, rapidly fastening her buttons. The woman clenched her jaw, picked up a full glass of water from the desk, and smashed it against the wall.

I flinched and moved further away from her, eyeing the broken pieces of glass on the wet floor.

"I had plans for you to father my next child! I would have given you money, prestige, and shared businesses. We could have built an empire together!" Saira screamed in rage. "Instead, you chose a petty life with your little jewel. How could you do this to us, Julian? I loved you!"

"Saira, we were *never* in love! Keep the hell away from my family and me. I am not your business anymore."

"Whatever you wish, Julian. One day, you will regret choosing her over me. I am so much more than your beloved angel."

"Saira, remember what I said earlier about Damian? Alistair's offer still stands. All it takes is a phone call, and I'll give him what he needs to take full custody of your son. Don't forget."

I picked up my jacket, walked toward the door, and turned the doorknob.

"Oh, you wouldn't dare! You're a father now, so you wouldn't do it if you had an ounce of empathy," she screamed.

"I have empathy, Saira. The boy deserves to be with the better parent."

"Oh, Julian. Your pretty little project blinds you."

"Don't fuck with me, Saira. Go and join your buddies in hell!" I shook my head and opened the door.

"Julian, don't walk away from me, do you understand? You can't leave me like this! Julian, darling! You know I wouldn't hurt your precious gem!"

I didn't need to hear any more of the psychopath's prattle, so I left her office.

***

Later that evening, after a warm shower with Saph, I noticed a message on my phone. It was from Saira, who'd written two words:

>You win.

I forwarded the message to Alistair, who responded:

>This snake will bite back. I'm here to help. Remember that.

Chapter Twenty-Six
Her Blood is Thicker than Water

Julian
Sunday, December 10

"Are you experiencing any contractions yet, love?"

I crawled under the duvet to join my angel on our bed after a warm shower.

"Only Braxton Hicks contractions," she answered. "They're irregular and too infrequent to be real contractions."

"Do you think we can sneak a bit of sausage inside you?"

"Julian!"

Saph played the role of the coy, innocent maiden with me. Two can play that game. I pressed my naked cock against her bare buttocks, spooning into my nude nymph.

"Come on, love. It may be the last time before the baby comes, and for another six weeks, according to the doc."

"Julian?"

"Yes, love."

"I need you now." Her warm fingers played with my teasing hand, which explored her body.

I smiled, kissed her neck, and flicked her taut and engorged nipples. Her breasts were generous, thanks to the pregnancy.

"Your nipples are so full and lush," I whispered into her ear.

Naked and pregnant, Sapphire was exotic, erotic, and beautiful.

"You've fathered my child, Julian. Should I start calling you 'daddy'?" The hot fox teased.

"You can call me 'daddy' any time." I nipped her earlobe, giving her smooth buttock a light smack.

My cock prodded her anus—it was virgin territory that I planned to invade in the future.

"Am I hurting you?" I asked, rubbing her nipple with my finger.

"No. Your touch feels so good, Julian."

"I read that it's worth stimulating a few hormones to help ripen your cervix. Oxytocin is one of them, isn't it?"

"Yes, dear. It's often called the love hormone."

"Aah! In that case, we're making love tonight." I fingered her pussy with three fingers. "Do you want a perineal massage, love?"

I'd given Saph perineal massages to stretch and increase flexibility in the perineum to prepare for the birth.

"We did a massage last night, Julian. I want your cock tonight."

Saph used the hard knob of my dick to stroke her slippery clit. It slid readily between her vaginal lips, slick against the silky wetness, until it met the heat of her clit. My arm circled her waist to hold her in position before my hardened cock drove into her.

"You love this, don't you?" I panted, never letting up my rhythm for the moment.

"Yes, Julian. I love this so much! Please, go faster!" Saph begged, as her walls clenched around my stiff dick.

I growled into her ear, tightening my grip on her girth, and the sheer animal excitement of the moment pushed her over the edge, where she cried in her climax. I joined her, matching her cries, and releasing my cum until I shuddered and loosened my grip on her. Time stood still, and all we were aware of was this moment of pleasure.

Saph cuddled into my chest, breathing me in. "You smell so good, Julian."

"So do you, Saph."

I inhaled her natural fragrance, which proved to be an intoxicating experience, like a drug, and I had done my fair share of drugs in a past life. The clandestine sex parties hosted by Saira, where cannabis, opiates, and cocaine were readily available, were a distant memory of the past.

"Darling, your son is frantically kicking. He's ready to come out soon," Saph said.

She placed my hand on the left side of her large bump, where I felt our child move repeatedly. "That's his kicking spot right there," she whispered, grinning from ear to ear.

"It's beautiful, Saph. We made this happen."

"We did, Julian. We made this family."

Monday, December 11

Drake Octavius Richland weighed 7.5 pounds and measured 20.8 inches long when he was born at 7.23 p.m. on Monday, December 11.

Saph had started her contractions at around one in the morning, only a few hours after we'd fucked. The contractions grew stronger and more intense as the hours flew. By sunrise, we were in a private room in the maternity wing of Saint John's Hospital, with a view overlooking the harbor and the ocean.

"How often do we get to watch the sunrise?" Saph joked in between contractions, as we watched the hot sun ascend while its warm hues lit the cold sky.

The medical staff gave her a much-needed epidural in the afternoon to ease the pain after her water broke. I felt sorry for my angel, but I knew she was strong—she was going to pull through just fine. After all, her blood is thicker than water.

By 6.47, Saph was kneeling on all fours on the bed—a position the midwife recommended to help with the birth. The midwife and her assistant were in the room with us.

"Tell me you love me, Julian!" Saph screamed, when another agonizing contraction hit her hard.

"I love you, Saph. You are doing amazing, you hear me? I love you!" I squeezed her hand and rubbed her shoulder.

Sapphire endured more than eighteen hours of bone-crunching labor. With the midwife's help, I cut the umbilical cord and was the first parent to hold our son, who let out a good cry, while the midwife's assistant stitched a small perineal tear that Saph had. Afterward, when Saph was resting on her back, I placed our child on her bare chest. The front of her hospital gown was unbuttoned, allowing the baby to bond skin-to-skin and become familiar with his mother's scent.

"He takes after his father." She smiled as tears of joy rolled down her face. Her hair was matted, and the outline of her face was damp with sweat.

"Here, love." I took a tissue from the bedside table and gently wiped her face.

"Julian, thank you. Thank you for our son," Saph murmured, holding Drake, who fell asleep.

After alerting our families of Drake's birth, my mother was the first one to visit us. Sadly, Saph's family failed to respond.

"Well, look at this little fella! He's so beautiful, Saph!" Mom wept, nursing our bundle of joy.

"He has his father's dark hair and eyes," Saph commented, smiling at Mom.

"He reminds me of Julian when he was born," Mom declared, grinning like the proud grandmother she was.

"Vera called and said she's on the way, but she's running late," I told Saph, taking Drake from Mom.

"Oh, that's typical of Vera. She's always late. Honey, you're holding my grandson like a pro." Mom watched the way I cradled my boy.

Drake yawned, and his tiny fingers uncurled, before curling again. His skin was still pink from the birth, and he had a little cap to keep his head warm. The little guy was snug in his tiny yellow bodysuit, which Saph had bought a week before the birth.

"You remind me of your father." Mom's eyes were red with bittersweet tears.

I missed my old man, and I wished to God that he was still alive to see Drake.

After a few minutes, Mom kissed Saph's forehead and said, "I'm going to love you and leave you, my angels. I will be back tomorrow afternoon."

"I'll see you tomorrow, Mom."

"Are you taking time off work, Julian?" My mother asked.

"I've already let work know that I'm taking the next two weeks off," I responded. "I've called Saph's employer, and she's officially on parental leave."

I winked at Saph, who grinned at me.

Sapphire

"Heeeyyy! I can't believe I'm an aunt! Congratulations, you two!" Vera hugged her brother, then came to my side as I rested on the bed. "I'm sorry for being late. I was caught up in a meeting on the way." She blushed, averting her eyes from Julian.

"You just missed your mom, but I'm glad you're here!" I exclaimed.

We both squealed and clapped our hands, while Julian groaned.

"Where's my nephew?" Vera looked around, then spotted our son asleep in his bassinet. "Oh, he's so adorable!" she gasped. "He's the perfect combination of both of you!"

Vera placed a small teddy bear near his tiny feet, handed me a bouquet of fresh flowers, and gave Julian a shaving kit.

"I thought you'd need the kit, not that you'll use it much." Vera chuckled at Julian, who scowled.

"I prefer ruggedly handsome than the pretty boy look." I smiled at my man, who folded his arms in confidence and smirked at his sister.

"Jules was a pretty boy in high school before he bulked up," Vera revealed.

"Pretty boy? Nah!" Julian shook his head while Vera nodded hers.

"You're a tough woman, Saph. Julian messaged me that the labor lasted over eighteen hours. Shit!" Vera sat on the bed and held my hand.

"I'm glad it's over," I confessed. "Julian was a real hero. He didn't flinch or faint, and he was as cool as a cucumber."

"Ice cold, more like it! He's a flipping ice cube," Vera teased her brother, who rolled his eyes.

I changed the subject, focusing on Vera. "How have you been, Vera? Congratulations on your new job as one of Orion's best in-house lawyers."

"Thanks, Saph. I'm loving it!" Her eyes sparkled. She'd started working for the artificial intelligence software company which provided services for oil and gas operators worldwide.

Her aura spoke volumes that it was more than just her job that gave her a new glow—her cheeks were flushed. I was curious to learn more about Vera's "glow", but I couldn't do that with Julian in the same room.

"Julian, do you mind if I have a minute alone with your sister?"

"Why? There's nothing you need to hide from me." Julian's forehead creased, while one eyebrow cocked.

"It's not always about me, darling." My eyes darted at Vera, before returning to Julian's stare.

"Fine. I'll ask the nurses if they have a vase for the flowers." He took the bouquet from my lap and walked out of the room.

"Alright, Vera. This is just between you and me now. Are you seeing someone new?"

She tucked her chin and bit her lip.

"You are! Who is he?"

"Don't tell Julian."

"I won't say anything if you promise me he's treating you well."

"He's very different to the asshole I dated once."

"Who is this new man, Vera?"

"His name is Alistair. Alistair Scott."

Oh. My. Lord. Alistair funded Paul McGrath's last election campaign.

"*The Alistair Scott?* This guy is one of Lester Harbor's business celebrities! Hey, isn't he on the board of directors for Orion?"

Vera played with her necklace, leaned her head back, and let out a deep sigh.

"Yeah, about that. It's a company his family has invested in for years. He's a professional investor in the energy and petroleum sector and in real estate."

"Vera, sweetie, I hope you know what you're doing with this man," I said.

"Promise me you won't tell Julian yet," Vera begged.

"Why?"

"Because I need to tell him. You see, Alistair is Saira's ex-husband. Julian is aware of that and he's protective about who I date."

"Oh, goodness. Julian is going to skewer you alive, Vera!"

"It's not what you think. Alistair hates Saira."

"Vera, don't let him use you."

"Oh, he won't use me. Alistair cares for me a great deal, and he wants to protect my family."

"Vera, Alistair wants full custody of his son. He knows Julian can help him, and it's more than just a coincidence that you're his sister. Julian's trying to play his cards right, and Saira's agreed to back off. So, don't let Alistair use you to aggravate war against Saira through Julian."

"Saph, he's not malicious like Saira. I know he wants full custody of his son, and there are excellent reasons for that. However, he's a man of empathy, and Julian knows this too."

"I think Saira will leave us alone, Vera. Julian's words are strong and are not to be taken lightly." I folded my arms and sighed.

"For now. If it were up to Alistair and me, we would strike the snake while the rod is still hot before the snake bites the heel," Vera pointed out.

Perhaps she was right, but I had just given birth and wanted to celebrate life with my partner and child. The last thing I wanted to do was to get my hands dirty and finish off the snake. There was a time and place for everything in due time.

"Be careful, Vera. We're at peace right now," I warned my friend.

"With Saira, there's no such thing as peace. That's what Alistair said. Believe me, he genuinely wants to help you and Julian," Vera said.

Interesting.

I wondered if Vera had met a man who loved her just as much as Julian loved me.

"So, is Alistair your boyfriend?"

"Yes."

"When do I meet him, and when will you tell Julian?"

"Soon."

Vera's face radiated with the brilliance of a love story that had a bright future.

Chapter Twenty-Seven
Fire and Ice

Sapphire
Saturday, October 6, ten months later

"Saph, I can't find my socks!"

"Have you tried checking the laundry room?" I suggested.

"Where the fuck are my socks? Why aren't they in here?" Julian stormed out of the walk-in wardrobe.

"Scowling isn't going to make your socks appear, darling."

"I knew it was a bad idea to get rid of Nadia."

"Oh, you mean the cleaner you used to fuck occasionally before you fully committed yourself to me? No wonder your apartment was spotless," I retorted, with a dash of sarcasm.

I'd met Nadia once by accident during the early days of dating Julian—I'd arrived at his apartment one hour early. I wasn't surprised to see her in a kinky French maid's outfit with a vacuum in one hand.

Julian had his way with women, to say the very least.

"Nadia kept things in order, which is a lot more than I can say about this ... dump!" Julian hissed, shaking his head with fury.

"You know what, Julian? I've got news for you. Things get messy. We have a baby, and it's not easy because life is a messy pile of everything!"

"Wow, do you want a medal for that, Saph?"

"Yeah! Maybe I do! When Drake gets sick, and you're traveling for work, I don't get any sleep. Then I spend half my day waiting at the doctor's reception to check if he has another ear infection."

"You're off work! You can't complain that life is so hard when I bring in the family income. Do you know how hard I work for this family?"

I stalked into the bathroom and locked the door for a minute of peace, away from an angry Julian, who couldn't stand it if one single thing was out of place in the house. My boyfriend was an obsessive neat freak. I'd taken parental leave from work to stay home with Drake for at least a year, so life had taken a dramatic turn for me. Having a baby had certainly changed my lifestyle. Gone were the days when I slinked in gorgeous dresses at evening cocktail parties. I stared at the mirror and saw a shadow of myself. My unwashed hair was in a ponytail, and I wore gray sweatpants.

After Drake's birth, I lost most of the weight that I'd gained during my pregnancy. However, I couldn't shake off the last six pounds, which were attached to my hips like a spare tire, no matter how much I exercised or how little I ate. My breasts weren't as perky as they used to be, and they sagged slightly lower after I stopped breastfeeding. My nipples were more prominent and would remain that way. On the skin of my lower abdomen I had a few stretch marks, which had appeared when I was pregnant.

Julian, on the other hand, had become more toned and well-defined. He reminded me of a Cabernet Sauvignon, made to last with age.

Our sex life had taken a nosedive after Drake's birth. Consumed by sleepless nights, thanks to a child who didn't sleep well, and exhausting days, the last thing I wanted was to dress up in some kinky outfit for a man who complained that the house was messy.

I was not Nadia.

"Saph? Open the door, please. I'm sorry, I haven't been fair to you."

"Julian, you're not getting any sex today, so don't think you can charm your way into my panties."

"Not even a little make-up sex?"

"Drake will wake up from his nap soon."

"We can make it quick and dirty."

Tempting.

"When's your mom coming to take Drake?"

"Tomorrow. We can have a lazy Sunday and catch up on some good loving."

I rolled my eyes, sighed, then unlocked and opened the bathroom door.

"One hour." I stared at him.

"Huh?"

"We've got one hour before your son wakes up. Take your pants off now!" I commanded, gently pushing Julian's chest.

"But I thought you said Drake wakes—"

"In one hour!" I playfully pinched Julian's ass. "Do you want me or not?"

We moved to the bed and frantically removed each other's clothes in aching lust and need. It had been a long time since we'd made love, and our hunger for each other was insatiable. Julian opened the drawer by his bedside and whipped out a string of anal beads and a tube of lubricant. He lubricated each bead while massaging my anal hole. We had talked about using the beads for a long time, and I was ready now.

"That's it, love. Straddle me." Julian held onto my hips with both hands as I sat across his naked thighs.

I stared intensely at my lover while my heart pounded with excitement as he inserted the lubricated beads, one by one, into my anus with care. He cocked his head to one side and stared at me with a hint of angelic innocence; his irises were almost indistinguishable from his pupils. I inhaled his familiar musky scent and glided my fingers along his smooth, tan skin.

"Sapphire, I want you to feel comfortable about this," Julian murmured, stroking my ass cheek with one hand, while the other hand controlled the string of love beads. "Tell me if it hurts."

I gasped as my body took in the new sensation of the beads. Each bead on the string was bigger than the previous one that he'd placed inside me. His ravenous, dark eyes, which glinted with delight, drilled through my soul. "Does it hurt, darling?" he asked, gently pushing another bead through my anal hole.

"It feels tense, yet my body wants more," I replied, hugging his body.

"Relax. You can trust me."

"I trust you."

"Let my cock come inside your pussy." His deep voice rumbled as his warm breath sent electric shivers down my spine. I took a deep breath and followed Julian's instruction, while he continued kissing my neck.

"Bingo. I found you," I murmured, feeling the tip of his cock at my entrance. I plunged down, giving his thick shaft an immediate and deep entry into my juicy sex.

"Fuck! Your cunt is so warm and snug." Julian's breath was hot on my skin. He continued using the beads to stimulate the nerves inside my anus while I screwed his throbbing cock and moaned with aching need.

"Stop right there," I whispered as my body adjusted to the heated sensation of the gentle anal penetration. "I like this."

"Do you want to know a secret, my love?" Julian asked. His stiff dick rewarded my inner walls with a deeply stimulating, hot massage.

"What's your secret, darling?" I clung onto him, moving back and forth in unison. His cheeks were flushed, and droplets of sweat ran down his temples.

"You're the first woman and the only woman I've ever loved." His breathing grew heavier when we thrust into each other. He stroked the curve of my hips and waist, triggering me to throw my head back and cry out as our rhythmic lovemaking continued.

"You feel so amazing," I whispered into Julian's ear, rocking forward and moving my hips at a steady pace.

"Oh, God, Saph. I want this so much," Julian groaned, as the thrusting became faster and rougher. I squeezed my inner muscles as I rode up and down him, enjoying the satisfaction of his thick cock combined with the anal beads.

"Fuck, Saph. I can't hold it back any longer," he grunted, massaging inside my pussy with his meaty cock. He pushed deeper into me as I tightened my grip on his shoulders. His thrusts were greedy, speeding faster, while I rubbed against his pubic bone. All the while, the stimulating sensation of the beads contributed toward building my climax.

"Oh, Julian! I'm going to cum!" I cried out. My heart pumped with excitement as I reached the pinnacle of being ravished. An orgasmic wave washed over my body as I yelled out my lover's name. *My Julian!*

"That's it, love. That's it," he groaned, spanking my left ass cheek, then clutching it tight.

"I love you, Julian!" I cried.

"That's my love. Oh, God, Saph! I love you!" Julian shouted, then shuddered his release, letting his orgasm consume him.

After he'd removed the beads from my anus, we stared at each other, unveiling each other's souls through one gaze. Moments later, as we lay in bed, his eyes shone with happiness.

"I don't deserve you. Yet I belong to you," he whispered, nuzzling his face against mine.

Sunday, 11:00 a.m.

"Aww, who's the most handsome little man in town? Why, of course, you are!" Frances cooed with delight, as she held her grandson in her arms.

Drake responded by giggling, gurgling, and sticking his fingers in her mouth.

"Boo! Peek-a-boo!" Frances continued.

"Drake can be quite a handful," I commented.

"Oh, pooh! No grandchild of mine is too much to handle."

"We can pick him up from your place," Julian suggested.

"I'll drop him off." Frances's dark eyes commanded her son to listen to her.

"What time works for you? I asked.

"Seven. I'll be back at around seven, so you two crazy kids go and have some fun!" Frances grinned, revealing the same white teeth Julian showed when he smiled.

A few minutes later we stood by the window, watching Frances strap Drake in the baby seat in the back of her car.

"I ought to thank Frances for taking our son out today. Honestly, I would go insane without her." I beamed at Julian.

"She loves to spend quality time with her grandson." Julian's eyes crinkled with a smile.

"Indeed she does. I'm forever grateful to have Frances as my family."

"She's as much your mother as she's my mother, love."

I stared at Julian like a love-struck teenager. Sometimes, when we argued, I felt like throwing a shoe at his face. At other times, he brought the moonlight to my dark winter evenings and the sunshine to my frosty days.

"Come here, babe." I cupped my hands on Julian's jaw, pulled him closer, and buttered his lips with a smooth, warm kiss.

"Mmm, now we're talking," he replied between kisses.

He maneuvered his groin against my pelvis and craftily massaged my buttocks with his expert hands.

"What are we going to do today?" I clasped my hands around his neck and shoulders.

"It's a surprise. Get your winter coat and your gloves on."

"Oh?"

"You'll find out soon."

Julian's wicked grin said enough.

***

About forty-five minutes later, I felt like a deer on ice.

Yes, that's right.

Ice.

"Julian, don't let go!" I yelped, clinging onto my man as if my life depended on him in the crowded indoor ice rink. I'd swapped my sturdy shoes for a rental pair of thin blades that barely kept me steady on the cold, hard ice.

"You've got to bend your knees a little and keep your weight on the base of your feet," Julian instructed.

"Lord have mercy on my body and soul if I let go of you," I wailed as Julian gently pushed me away from the edge of the rink.

"Now, I'm taking you further into the middle, and we're going to have a little fun." Julian's smile warmed me up in the glacial skating hall, encouraging me to move away from the railing and further into the crowd of skaters. "Hold my hand, love, and enjoy," he encouraged.

"I'm trying, Julian," I replied, slowly gliding along the ice with my blades.

Then it happened.

All it took was a slight imbalance and loss of control, causing my bottom to smack on the ice.

"Up we go! Come on," Julian insisted, lifting me and bringing me close against the warmth of his body. Holding my hand, he took the lead, and we glided together to the side of the rink, where I took short steps out of the ice and onto the rubber mat.

"Do you need a short break?" Julian asked, as we sat on the bleachers.

"Yes. I need a cup of coffee." I threw my head back and laughed as my eyes twinkled at his soulful gaze.

"Alright, I'll grab something for us to drink." His eyes focused on the kiosk to the right. "I'll be back soon."

I loosened the laces of my ice skates and rubbed my ankles, which were now free from the uncomfortable tightness. I continued massaging my ankles and lower shins, before looking up to a sight that I dreaded. Jessie Caruso, the woman who hated me, was standing next to Julian in the queue at the kiosk, catching up on old times. She was playing with her hair and had captured his eyes with ambitious intensity. Each time he spoke, she laughed on cue. Then, she touched his arm. I noticed that he flinched, but the woman was invading my man's territory. I removed the ice skates from my feet, tied the laces, and held them tightly as I got up from the bench and marched toward them. Fire burned up inside me in the chilly ice hall.

"Hey, Jessie! It's been a while. How have you been?" I tilted my head, flipped my hair to one side, and stroked Julian's arm.

Jessie wore a tiny leopard-print top and low-rise jeans, and she looked fitter than ever. Her breasts bounced as she rolled her hips, angling into Julian.

She was a woman on the prowl.

"Meow! Look what the cat dragged in," the bitch sang.

"Meow yourself," I spat back. "Aren't you cold?"

"It's freezing in here! Julian and I were catching up on old times," the cat purred.

"Jessie, I had no idea you enjoyed ice skating." Julian raised his left eyebrow, while slipping his hand in my back pocket and gently massaging my buttock in circular motions.

"You never took me skating, honey." Jessie pulled a trout pout.

"A lot has happened since we last spoke, Jessie. Saph and I are a family now, and we've got a child."

"A kid? You? Wow!" Jessie cupped her mouth in surprise. She then turned toward me, slit her eyes, and smirked. "My, I can tell. Saph, weren't you thinner when we first met? You've packed on quite a few pounds," Jessie sneered, gazing at my hips.

"I'm not plastic fantastic—" I began, but Julian jumped in.

"Saph looks great. I love a woman with natural curves." He showed off his playboy grin and squeezed my ass.

I felt a slight twinge of jealousy as I looked first at Julian, who was chiseled like a marbled wonder crafted by Michelangelo, then at his well-proportioned ex.

They had great sex together, Wicked Anxiety declared. Her eyes were the same color as mine—sapphire.

She's a remnant of his past, Lady Hope challenged her wretched sister, caressing her snow-white hair.

Jessie is beautiful. You have let yourself go, my little dumpling. Julian will return to his old ways. Wicked Anxiety let out a sinister laugh and clicked her manicured fingers.

Saph, don't let anyone walk over you. Lady Hope patted my arm, then turned to her sister. *Sapphire will always be beautiful. Leave her alone, sister!*

Both entities faded as Jessie faced me with a seething anger that surfaced like hot lava.

"You're a mother. Good luck." She masked a plastic smile.

"You're next in the queue, Jessie. We'll see you around," Julian said.

"You will see me around. I've accepted a job as the new receptionist at the university's archaeology department."

"How on earth?" I asked.

"Oh, let's say a certain someone who funds the department spoke with the human resources manager. I needed a job, and I wanted to work in a place where I know a familiar face or two."

Julian just shook his head—he was holding back words he couldn't use in a public place where there were kids around. "I don't believe this," he muttered, teeth clenched. "I'm surprised they never notified me. I'll talk to HR on Monday."

"See you on Monday, Jules." Jessie waved her fingers and flashed a smile at him. She narrowed her eyes at me before turning her back on us to order her coffee.

5:00 p.m.

Julian and I rested in the bathtub, soaking our tired bodies. His hands massaged my shoulders, and his thumbs moved along the blades in circular motions.

"What the fuck were they thinking, hiring someone who can barely use an Excel spreadsheet, let alone find her way to the printer room?" Julian asked.

"Do you think Saira is behind this?" I played with the soap bubbles that floated on the water.

"Most likely."

"What are you going to do about it?"

"If it's Saira, she's looking for some overdue attention. I won't give her that."

"Hmm. She's dangerous."

"Don't worry, love. If she causes more trouble, I know what to do. Trust me."

Julian kissed the back of my head and ran his hands along my arms.

"Alistair can help, Julian," I suggested.

True to Vera's words, Alistair was a man who showed empathy and respect. We'd met on a few occasions, including at Vera's birthday dinner, and he'd bonded well with Julian.

"We'll get through this," Julian assured me, kissing my wrist.

We were hopeful, but we weren't prepared for the heartbreak that lurked like a callous mugger with a knife, hiding in the shadows of the night.

Chapter Twenty-Eight
Stolen

Julian
One month later

Pick up the phone, Saph. Pick it up.

Finally she took the call.

"Hello?" I said

"Happy birthday, sexy," Saph drawled.

"I'm going to be late, love."

"Oh? That's highly unusual. What's up? It's seven o'clock on Friday night, and I'm already at the restaurant."

"It's Jessie."

"Oh."

A long pause followed.

"Darling? Are you still there?"

"Yeah, I'm here. What has Jessie done to make you prioritize her over your birthday dinner with me?"

"She claims she's going to kill herself."

"WHAT? Julian, she's manipulating you!" Saph shrieked.

"I know her," I explained. "She tried before when we were together. I need to go over there to make sure she doesn't hurt herself."

"Hurt herself?"

"Saph, she self-harms. That's all I'll say. Have a glass of wine and an appetizer. I promise I'll be there as soon as I sort this shit."

"Julian? Call professional help for her when you get to her place. She's not your problem anymore."

7.24 p.m.

"Jessie? OPEN UP!"

"Juuulian, is that you?" Jessie slurred, opening her apartment door. "Juuulian! Oh, Juuulian!" She sang, swirling around in her red silk kimono.

The apartment stank of cannabis and Jessie's eyes were bloodshot.

"Show me your wrists," I ordered.

"No!"

"Show me your wrists!"

She slowly turned her wrists up, revealing a crisscross of old, faded scars.

I rushed to the bathroom and saw the sink was clean.

"Won't you stay for a drink?" Jessie purred.

"You lied!" I hissed.

"What? NO! I swear. I was lonely, and these thoughts—these thoughts, they just appeared in my head, like a swerve of anxiety hit me!"

"Shut up!"

"Juuu Juuu ... Please! I felt so alone! I'm so alone in this world!" The woman sobbed and ran her hands through her wild, blonde hair. She was a mess, and I couldn't just stand there.

Shit.

"Come here, Jessie." I took her hand, and she wrapped her arms around me. I let her bury her face in my chest, which she stained with her tears.

About fifteen minutes later, we were sitting on her sofa drinking sodas while reminiscing about the days when we dated.

"Remember that New Year's Eve party when Vera refused to talk to me?" Jessie crossed her legs and shifted closer to me.

I placed my nearly-empty glass of soda on the table and looked at my watch. It was seven forty-five, and I needed to leave.

"Yeah, I remember that." I suddenly felt drunk, despite not drinking an ounce of alcohol.

"Vera never liked me, did she?" Jessie muttered.

My vision started to blur, and the room began to spin.

"Julian?"

I tried to focus on the conversation, but I was struggling to concentrate.

"Saph?" I needed my angel.

"I'm Jessie, darling. Saph's not here."

Through my blurred vision and drowsiness, I watched Jessie remove her kimono and reveal her bare skin. A shadow moved from the bedroom into the living room. Someone else was in the apartment, and I recognized his muscled body.

"What the fuck—? I'm losing control ..." I mumbled, surrendering to the sweet slumber.

Sapphire
8.15 p.m.

I thought we were happy. I was fucking wrong. It wasn't enough, because our love was never enough for the world. All it took was one video sent to my phone for my world to fall apart. It was a fifteen-second video of a real-life Barbie sucking my man's cock. That Barbie was Jessie Caruso. And that man was Julian Richland.

"Checkmate," she announced, before the film clip ended.

It wasn't an old video, because he'd worn the same shirt that morning.

"One more for the road, Jack!" I hiccupped, pointing at my empty wine glass to the waiter.

Tonight was the night I'd planned to surprise Julian by proposing to him.

"Saph? What are you doing here all alone?" A handsome man in a gray, single-breasted suit stood in front of me.

"Raphael? What are you doing here?"

"I just finished dinner with one of McGrath's old pals. How about you?"

"I'm just sitting here, about to get wasted! Care to join me?" I gave a crooked smile.

"How many drinks have you had?" Raphael sat on the empty chair where Julian should have been.

"Two."

"Who's taking care of your kid tonight?"

"Julian's mom. Drake's staying at her place for the weekend."

"I suppose another drink won't hurt." Raphael grinned.

"Here you go, ma'am." Jack handed me a glass of Pinot noir.

"Excuse me, I'll have another one of those," Raphael instructed the waiter, who nodded his head.

"You know, Julian calls this red wine *Vitis vinifera Pinot noir.*" I raised my wine glass and nodded my head with approval.

"He's quite a fancy guy." Raphael chuckled.

"He's an intellectual snob, at best," I replied. "Do you know that he failed half the students in one of his classes last semester? Half, as in fifty percent!"

"Shit! I did not know that."

Then I lost it. The tears rolled down my cheeks at a rapid rate.

"Saph, what's the matter? Hey, look at me." Raphael pulled his chair closer to me and put one arm around me. "Hey, Saph. Talk to me. Tell me what happened."

"The bastard cheated on me." I took my mobile phone from my purse and showed Raphael the video of Jessie feasting on my man's cock.

"Sir, here is your wine." Jack arrived at our table and placed the wine glass near Raphael.

A few minutes after polishing off our glasses, I paid the bill, and we went for a walk outside. I felt giddy, flirty, and reckless.

Reckless was the best word to describe the mood of the night, as it started to drizzle with the November rain.

"I waited at the restaurant, but he never came. Instead, his ex-girlfriend sent me that disgusting video," I lamented.

"Nasty!" Raphael winced.

"On his birthday! It's his goddamn birthday! How could he?"

"I always knew that guy was scum. I'm sorry."

"Sorry doesn't take the pain away." I wiped a tear that rolled down my cheek.

"Hey, come here. Let those tears out. I'm here for you."

With those kind words of comfort, I caved into Raphael's sweet embrace. His woody scent reminded me of what we'd once had. I looked up, and his eyes were hazy with want. All it took was one look, and his lips descended on mine.

His lips. Not *Julian's* lips.

"Stop! I can't do this!" I cried, sobering up. I pulled myself away from Raphael's body and wiped his moist imprint off my mouth. The evening was already sour, and we'd made it worse with a stolen kiss. I looked at Raphael, who smirked a player's smile, and I knew that something was wrong. Horribly wrong.

Wicked Anxiety stood in front of me and shook her head.

Use your logic, Saph. The man is lying to you about everything. Her perfectly manicured hands rested on her hips.

"Who do you work for?" I demanded.

"Come on, Saph! You know I don't play games."

"Bull fucking shit! Who do you really work for? I'm not talking about Paul!"

Furious with rage, I slapped Raphael's beautiful face. There. That wiped the smirk off his face.

"Answer my question, Raphael!"

"I believe you've met her already." The cunning prick's eyes twinkled.

"Saira Quinn. I should have known. Were you paid too?" I laughed in disbelief, gazing at the stars before I glared at Raphael.

"You know, everything always comes with a price," he said.

"If you have any compunction or decency left in your soul—"

I couldn't hold it together any longer. My knees began to shake, and I lost control. My body slumped to the ground, and I unleashed a lifetime of sorrows. After a minute of watching me cry, Raphael extended his hand to lift me off the ground.

"Saph, I've had enough." He closed his eyes and sighed.

"Piss off!" I barked, staring at the boats by the harbor.

"No, I'm serious. I can't keep hurting you," Raphael assured. "After your boyfriend ended his gig with Saira, she signed a contract with me. I had a college debt and—"

"Yada, yada, yada. I've heard this sob story before. Saira paid your debt and brought you into the world of politics, where you'll pursue your dream to become a leader of the free world one day."

Raphael surrendered to me with a weak smile.

"Is she friends with the senator?" I asked.

"No. However, a buddy of the senator owed her a favor. The rest is history."

"Raphael, did Saira ask you to sleep with me?" I narrowed my eyes at him.

His empty stare and the long silence said it all.

"Was our relationship ever real?" I dared to ask.

"I was falling for you, but it was already too late for me."

"Too late for you?"

"Julian had you at first sight, and he never let go."

"Raphael, what do you know about a woman named Jessie Caruso?"

"Jessie Caruso. Ah, yes. The woman in the video."

"How do you know her?"

"Saph, you don't want to know."

"Do I look like I'm in fucking kindergarten? Tell me, Raphael, before I sell your soul to the other devil!"

"What do you mean?"

"Alistair Scott happens to be my best friend's lover. He would kill for her and her family. Do you know who my best friend is?"

Raphael shook his head.

"She is my son's aunt and Julian's sister."

"Holy fucking hell! Fucking shit!" Raphael ran his fingers through his hair several times.

"All I have to do is make a phone call to my friend, and your political career will be dead. Alistair has been rather generous with funding Paul's campaign."

My mouth twitched upward into an evil grin. Wicked Anxiety stood firm by my side, blowing fear, like gusts of wind, into Paul's soul.

The guy shivered in anxiety as his blood turned cold.

The asshole finally relented. "Alright, alright! I'll tell you."

"Good." I couldn't stop grinning, while Wicked Anxiety nodded her head.

"Jessie and I fucked. We were paid to fuck while people watched us at Saira's private parties."

"Did you know Jessie was going to call Julian tonight?"

"Honest to God, no. Saira doesn't share her plans. She tells us what to do."

"So, you're a gopher." Unfolding my arms, I stepped forward into Raphael's space and met him eye to eye.

"She told me to find you at the restaurant and seduce you. She offered me a spot on the board of directors for a company she owns."

"And you believe her?" I chuckled. "If I were you, I would tread carefully as to whose side you want to be on."

Raphael wiped away a droplet of sweat that had landed on his brow. *He's dripping with fear.* Wicked Anxiety clapped her hands three times.

"Saph, I'm telling you the truth. She's secretive in her affairs with individuals. It's a case of the left hand not knowing what the right is doing," Raphael appealed.

I pulled out my phone and watched the video again. It just couldn't be possible that Julian would willingly risk everything, especially on the night of his birthday. This didn't make sense.

Raphael looked at the video as I replayed it. "Stop. Stop right there."

I paused the video and examined the scene. There was another man's hand behind Jessie as she played with Julian's cock. I never saw Julian's face throughout the entire segment of the film.

"Do you recognize the furniture? The place? Anything about the background?"

"It's Jessie's apartment," Raphael pointed out.

"If you have a soul left in you, Raphael, you will help me now!" I declared, heading toward the taxi rank on the main street.

I prayed to God, hoping that my man wasn't hurt. It was never too late to save someone. I was on my way.

Chapter Twenty-Nine
The Die is Cast

Sapphire

"Open the fucking door!" I banged my fists against the hard wooden door outside Jessie's apartment.

"Goddamn it! Open the door!" I yelled again.

"Step aside." Raphael shoved me away from the doorstep and knocked on the door.

Senior constable Constance Fraser, who'd met us outside the apartment building, remained silent. Vera was in Dubai for work when I called—naturally, she'd panicked about her brother's safety. Thankfully, Alistair had friends in the police department who'd sent Constance our way.

"Jessie? It's Raphael. You need to open the door now, sweetie. I'm here to help you."

I heard footsteps approach the door, which opened immediately.

"Raphael?" Jessie's bleary eyes cried to the man for help.

The girl's kimono hung off her shoulders, and the belt to wrap it was missing, exposing a round breast and tanned thighs.

"Step aside, Raphael." I pushed passed him, marched inside the apartment, and grabbed the maniac's shoulders.

"You fucking bitch!" I slammed her against the wall.

"Let go," Constance insisted.

"You're lucky the police officer is here to protect you." I pressed my hand against Jessie's throat, wishing I had a hunting knife to slice it.

"Where is *my man?*" My thumb stroked the beating pulse along Jessie's delicate neck.

Strangle her. Wicked Anxiety insisted while inspecting her perfect claws.

Tempting.

"Come, Saph. You heard the police. Let go." Raphael pulled me away from Jessie.

"You brought a fucking cop in here! Why, Raphael?" Jessie whined.

"The game is over, Jessie. Whatever Saira promised you, it's over," Raphael declared. He directed Jessie to sit on the sofa with him, making sure she didn't bolt toward the door.

Keeping her hand close to her holster, Constance searched the apartment for Julian. "Saph, he's in here!" Constance raised her hand in the air and signaled for me to follow her into the bedroom. "He's asleep."

Oh, my! My poor Julian! Seeing him half-naked on the bed broke my heart. Monsters came in all shapes and sizes, and Jessie was one of them. She appeared sexually attractive with the perfect pout, but she was crazy and harmful. That was the kind of monster she was.

"Julian! Wake up, darling. It's me, Saph." I picked up his boxer shorts from the floor and put them on him.

Julian stirred from his sleep. "Mmm, Saph? I don't feel well." His eyes revealed a world of darkness and vulnerability.

I glanced at Constance, who made a full sweep of the room and entered the bathroom to see if anyone else was in the apartment.

"The Henchman," Julian muttered, grabbing my wrist.

"Who?"

"He must've left. He was here before I fell asleep."

"Who is he?"

"A sadistic man who works for Saira. I didn't realize he and Jessie were acquainted."

"I know what she did to you."

"What? How?"

"Jessie filmed a snippet of what happened and sent it to me."

"This is fucked. I never thought ..."

I brought Julian's head to my chest and felt the warmth of his tears spill on my dress. "You were assaulted against your will."

"I'm so sorry, Saph. I'm so sorry."

"I'm sorry for you. It happens to men too, not just women." I released him from my caress and held his left hand.

Still drowsy, Julian sat up and lowered his head.

"All's clear!" Constance announced, stepping out of the bathroom.

"I'm going to be sick." Julian's face was pale and laced with sweat.

He leaned over and vomited on the floor, grasping my hand for comfort. Constance went into the bathroom and came back with tissues to wipe Julian's mouth.

"Take deep breaths, Julian. That's it. Breathe in deeply." She patted his back and glanced at me.

"I'll get some water," I suggested.

Fifteen minutes later, Constance left the apartment with Jessie in handcuffs. Raphael went with them, as he was needed for questioning at the police station. He winced and frowned—no doubt, he was worried about how this mess would affect his career in politics. Wicked Anxiety was by his side, accompanying him.

"I've called a cab to take you and Julian to the hospital," Constance said as she left. "They have staff who deal with this every week."

Two weeks later

On the night of the assault, the hospital doctor thoroughly checked Julian and typed a report for the police department. He found one bruise on Julian's shoulder—most likely from The Henchman. Julian was tested for sexually transmitted infections, and thankfully the results showed he was clean.

Jessie was charged with sexual assault and rape. She'd forced herself on Julian, giving him a blow job while he was defenseless and heavily sedated. She'd purposefully drugged him and caused him harm. Let's just say that orange would be her new color, with prison as her new home. The police tried to find The Henchman who'd assisted Jessie and kept Julian captive during the assault. He must have left town.

As for Raphael, McGrath fired him. The decision was made quickly when Julian and I were spending an afternoon with Vera and Alistair at his penthouse apartment. Alistair lived on the top two floors of an exclusive high-rise building in one of Lester Harbor's most expensive neighborhoods. He and Vera were a couple for a while now, so it was only natural for her to move in with him, making his apartment her home.

Drake was at his grandmother's house that day, so Julian and I could have a much-needed discussion with Alistair and Vera.

Vera was a flaming fireball of fury and persuaded Alistair to speak with Paul to replace Raphael with a more trustworthy advisor. "The guy played a hand in ruining my brother's life. Show him no mercy," she declared, placing her thumb down like a Roman emperor deciding a gladiator's fate in the arena of life.

"You are right, my darling." Alistair sat on his divan like a king on his throne. He picked up his cellphone and tapped a button. "Paul, it's me. Listen, I need you to do me a favor." Alistair put the phone on speaker mode, so we could all hear Paul.

"Yeah, what's up, Scotty?"

"You've got a fellow by the name of Raphael Thomas?"

"He's my advisor."

"Get rid of him. He's closely connected to someone who's scratching your opponent's back."

"Fuck."

"There's a saying along the lines of this: like an archer wounding all passersby, so is he who employs a fool."

"Machiavelli? Sun Tzu?"

"It's in the Bible, Paul. Proverbs 26:10."

"Scotty, I don't have time to memorize quotes." Paul chuckled.

Alistair uncrossed his legs and laughed. "Come on, Paul. You need to spend time being visible in your local church. The election's coming."

"I would if I could get more businesses to fund Saint Luke's Cathedral. The church would appreciate your generosity."

"Consider it done. The donation will be generous, and I expect publicity around it."

"Good. Now, about Raphael. Are you certain about his connections with Senator Colson?"

"Absolutely. Get rid of him."

"Consider it done. Thanks for the tip."

"That's what friends do, Paul."

Alistair hung up and placed the phone on the coffee table.

"Friends?" I questioned.

"There are no friends in business," Alistair replied.

Vera rubbed Alistair's shoulder and gazed at me. The two were majestic—she was Lester Harbor's new queen in business and politics, with Alistair as her partner.

The phone vibrated, and Alastair glanced at the screen. "Excuse me. I have to take this call." He took the phone and went into his home office.

"*Ad augusta per angusta,*" Julian murmured, sipping his coffee. "Vee, you're quite the eagle, rising to a high position and overcoming life's hardships," he continued, paraphrasing the Latin saying.

"Alistair wants full custody of Damian," Vera said. "It's an ongoing war between him and Saira. The boy suffers when he's with her."

"You're becoming attached," I commented, folding my arms.

"Alistair and Damian are my family too. They love me, and I love them," she said.

Julian got up from the sofa and paced in circles. None of us spoke for a while until he broke the ice.

"You're right." He frowned. "I told Saira to leave me alone, peace for peace. Now it's time for war."

Saira might be a snake, but Alistair was the eagle, with more power and connections than one could imagine. Now was the time to strike the snake.

"The eagle fights the snake in the air," I asserted. "It changes the battleground to where the snake has no power, making the snake weak."

"Very well, then. *Alea iacta est,*" Julian uttered.

"The die is cast," Vera declared.

We were at war.

Chapter Thirty
The Eagle and the Snake

Sapphire
One week later

"Sapphire."

"Saira."

The witch's steel-gray eyes met my sapphire-blue eyes.

"Haha, what a place to meet! I can see it's an acquired taste," Saira crowed, sniffing the air with disdain.

She dripped in high-end designer clothing from top to toe and had slung her white fur coat over her chair. We sat across each other at a modest airport café about forty minutes out of town. It was a domestic airport used less frequently these days.

"I appreciate that you came to meet me this afternoon," I declared, keeping my expression stone cold.

"Hmm, you have me itching with curiosity," Saira remarked. She looked around the airport, raised her eyebrows, and smirked. "Let's not beat around the bush, Sapphire. Shall we order a coffee?" Her eyes squinted at me.

"Actually, would you care to go for a walk with me? Julian's arriving from a short flight, and we should meet him."

"Julian is here?"

"He has a few words to say to you. We want to end this game of yours. Truthfully, we don't need war."

"Sapphire, what do you want? Do you want money? We can make a trade." The white witch's lips curved into an evil smile.

"Saira, we're willing to do whatever it takes." I clasped my hands.

"Well then, what are we waiting for? Lead the way, little one."

Saira irked me with her arrogance, but I had to keep my temper low and my head cool.

"Alright." I smiled, capturing Saira's sneaky sneer with my own eyes.

***

"I didn't know you had access through these gates," Saira commented, as I greeted Rupert, the smiling airport attendant.

"Come right this way, Miss Blake. Professor Richland is expecting you," Rupert said, opening the door to the airfield.

We followed Rupert, who led us across the tarmac toward a private jet, which was ready to welcome new passengers.

"Have a nice day, Miss Blake," Rupert chimed.

"Thank you, Rupert," I replied.

I remained silent as we walked up the steps and entered the jet. Saira, being a confident and proud woman, refused to show her fear. She followed me like an unsuspecting pig led for slaughter.

"Good afternoon, Miss Blake," the pilot greeted as the cabin door closed.

"Please take a seat, Saira," I instructed. "We're going to meet Julian soon."

"Oh? This will be quite an adventure," Saira laughed, with a wicked gleam in her eyes.

"Don't forget to buckle up," I replied.

I sat down, put on my seatbelt, and looked at Saira as we were about to take off.

"You surprise me. I'm starting to see why Julian chose you. You are full of adventure," she said.

I offered a simple smile—nothing more and nothing less.

After we were airborne and the seatbelt sign had switched off, I undid my seatbelt and stood. A flight attendant arrived with two drinks on her tray.

"Would you like something to drink, Saira? A cocktail, perhaps? Or a *soda?*"

I took both drinks from the tray and sipped one of the sodas. I offered the other glass to Saira.

"No, darling. Nothing for me."

"Oh? Why not?"

Saira's smile disappeared as the attendant returned to the back of the plane.

"Are you afraid that I might slip something in your drink?" I taunted. Her face turned ash white.

"Don't worry, dear Saira. I am cunning, but I am not callous."

"What do you want from me, Sapphire?" Saira snatched the glass I offered her.

"I want peace. And the only way I can find peace is by making sure you stay out of our lives for good."

"How do you intend to do that? I'm curious about the tricks you have up your sleeve," Saira cackled, unbuckling her seatbelt.

"Did you know that your Jessie Caruso drugged and raped Julian?" I questioned her.

"Oh my! I am shocked!" Saira clutched one of her jeweled hands to her chest. "I admit, I let her loose to have a little fun—it was a cat and mouse game. That was all."

"That cat and mouse game cost Julian his dignity. It left a scar that he and I share for the rest of our lives," I snapped, leaning over Saira.

The woman ignored my words, refusing to accept responsibility for the pain she caused.

"Where are you taking us, Sapphire? I'm curious," she drawled.

"Oh, we're just circling in the air," I replied. "A few of us are like eagles. We fly to catch our prey. You see, our prey are often predators."

"*We?* Excuse me?" Saira's eyes shot up.

She unbuckled her seatbelt and stood, turning her head quickly as she looked around the plane.

"Hello, Saira. It's been a while." Alistair stepped out from the back and strolled down the aisle. Not a hair was out of place on the man, who wore a simple dark suit, a gold Rolex watch, and black loafers.

The eagle meets the snake. Wicked Anxiety took a small bow.

"Alistair—" Saira's mouth dropped open as if she just saw a ghost.

I had unleashed Wicked Anxiety on Saira. The entity slithered toward the ash-blonde witch, grinning like a child who'd found a new toy.

"How are you, dear?" Alistair greeted Saira with a firm handshake, air-kissing one side of her head. He whispered something inaudible into her ear. Whatever he said had an impact on her. She froze like a statue and dropped her glass of soda on the floor.

A tall man appeared from the cockpit at the front of the plane. "Saira Quinn, I am lieutenant Frank Berry of the Montville State Police," the police officer announced, holding up his badge. "I am placing you under arrest on suspicion of illegal prostitution, drug trafficking, and the unlawful possession of drugs in your home. You are not obliged to say anything, but anything you say will be noted and may be used in evidence," he continued, handcuffing the witch.

"How c-c-could you? How could you do this to m-me?" she stammered, thrashing her head in bewilderment.

"All it took was one confession from Julian to Alistair, who has friends in the state police department," I explained. "While you've been here with me, they've been to your home and found enough evidence to place you under arrest."

"Saira, Julian *warned you not to fuck with him*. You believed you were untouchable. You were wrong." I folded my arms and shook my head.

"You bitch!" Saira screamed. The veins along her reddening neck began to pop out.

"You believed you were invincible. You were wrong," I continued.

"You believed you were smarter than Saph. That, my dearest Saira, is your downfall," Julian's voice boomed. He walked from the back of the plane with his hands in his pockets, stopped halfway down the aisle, and cocked his head to one side. "My, you have a grandiose sense of your ability," he added. "You play by using aggression and force. You have no feelings or emotions for people, and you show no remorse."

"JULIAN! After everything I have done for you!" Saira exploded, and tears fell down her face.

Yet, I felt no pity for her.

"Do you know what the police have found? Let me think." Julian raised his left knuckle and rested his chin on it. "The cocaine and mix of other drugs you keep in the cabinet near the kitchen, the books on your increasingly profitable underground prostitution ring, and the loaded gun you keep in the cupboard near Damian's room. My, you have been bad." Julian grinned.

"That is also more than enough evidence for a family court judge to remove any custody you have of your son," I added, darting my eyes at Alistair. Lady Hope stood by him, like a ray of light shining bright.

Alistair would have full custody of his son. Finally, after all these years. Lady Hope beamed.

"Saira, I have one more thing to say to you," I announced. "I'm not afraid of you, and I'm not afraid of telling you to go to hell. You'll feel right at home there."

"Ladies and gentlemen, please take your seats and put your seatbelts on. We are about to make a descent," the flight attendant announced.

Wicked Anxiety continued to stand near Saira. She winked at me and revealed a whip, ready to lash Saira's back. She wore an ominous smile—she was leaving me for Saira.

Julian
Three days later

How do you recover from a vicious assault? We know that the body heals, but we must remember that the mind and heart are equally strong. We do not grieve, for we find joy in love. Especially when you love someone as you love your soul. It's the kind of love that never stops even after the heart ceases to beat. No human power can break the love that Saph and I have.

"Do you know how much I adore you, Saph?" I murmured, playing with her chestnut hair as we lay in bed after some tender lovemaking.

"I know you love me, Julian, and I love you too." My angel smiled while her head rested on the pillow.

"You are my blue-eyed gem with the sweetest smile." I kissed her forehead and breathed in the aroma of fresh flowers—her fragrance.

Ah, the scent of jasmine on our bedsheets. I couldn't get enough of her.

"Oh, Julian. You are the essence of my heart. You keep the fire burning in my soul," she professed, touching my chest.

"I believe that our souls fused together the moment we met. This love of ours is so beautiful and powerful." My fingers caressed my darling's perfect face.

"With this love, we made a child, a home, and a family," she whispered.

"We did, darling. We certainly did."

Chapter Thirty-One
Galatea and Pygmalion

Sapphire
One year later

Not all relationships survive the four seasons, especially beyond spring's fair-weather sunshine. Some couples stay together, while others grow apart. Yet, life is full of surprises. I arrived alone at Vera and Alistair's engagement party at City Hall's grand ballroom. The couple planned to marry in a few months, then move to Dubai with Damian. The celebration was spectacular, with the city's elite rubbing shoulders, while the paparazzi waited at the red carpet outside, snapping photos of the rich and famous. I felt at home in an Egyptian blue, satin halter gown that displayed an eye-popping plunge down the front of my chest.

"You only live once, and you want Julian to notice you," Vera had said, when she'd twisted my arm into buying the daring evening dress a few weeks before.

After handing in my invitation at the door, I was finally inside the crowded ballroom, which was filled with all the glitz, glamor, and action that the city could muster. I scanned the room and found two familiar faces. Surrounded by a mob of sycophants, Vera and Alistair had mastered the art and business of socializing at high profile events.

"Saph! Over here!" Vera waved at me. She was a goddess in her strapless, silver gown.

I made my way toward her, grabbing a champagne glass from a cocktail waiter's drink tray.

"Darling, we haven't seen you in a while. Where on earth have you been?" Vera squeezed me tight.

Alistair nodded his head at me, then continued talking to Lester Harbor's mayor.

"I've been working for the circus, doing a juggling act between managing a career and embracing motherhood," I replied.

Vera grinned, then announced, "Julian is here. Look straight ahead."

My heart stopped beating for a second. Dressed in a black tuxedo, with his hair slicked back, the handsome devil took my breath away. "I expected your brother would be here, Vera." I smiled, eyeing his broad shoulders and athletic physique.

"She's trying to get her claws on him," Vera whispered, glaring at an attractive brunette chatting with Julian next to an ice sculpture.

"I see that," I sighed, slightly shaking my head.

"You should go over and talk to him."

"I will."

I felt waves of excitement rush from my gut to my heart as I walked toward Julian.

Breathe in and exhale, Saph. Lady Hope was there.

"Where's Wicked Anxiety?" I wondered aloud.

She's quite busy these days. Lady Hope smiled. *You can do it, Saph. That's it. Take one step closer. Now smile.*

My lips curled into a playful smile. Hope was always in my heart.

Julian's eyes locked with mine, before flickering back to the woman who held him captive in their conversation. He nodded at her, but there was no warmth in his eyes when he looked at her.

"Hello, stranger," I announced, rubbing my hand on his strong shoulder.

"Sapphire." Julian took my drink and sipped the champagne, before placing the glass on a table near the ice sculpture.

"Hi, I'm Sapphire Richland." I shook the woman's hand.

"Oh. I had no idea Professor Richland was married." She pursed her lips, refusing to reveal her name.

"Well, now you know," I quipped.

"Have a lovely evening, professor," she purred at him. She sneered at me before turning away to hunt her next prey.

"An old flame?" I asked Julian.

"She's not memorable." Julian's hand snaked around my waist, clenching it tight and close to him.

"You're late," he murmured, *sotto voce.*

"Sorry, darling. The hair and makeup artist took longer than expected," I replied, pecking his cheek with a kiss. His fresh aftershave unleashed a tantalizing scent of bergamot blended with lemon and cedarwood. I kissed his neck and jawline, tasting his delicious aroma of sensuality and sophistication.

"I've been waiting for you. Do you know what happens when a naughty angel keeps me waiting?" Julian murmured, with a mischievous gleam in his eyes.

"I want you," I whispered into his ear, as my body pressed against his. My breasts pushed into his chest while he rubbed my lower back. His fingers moved down to feel for a panty line.

"No thong?" he murmured.

I felt the warmth of his minty breath on my skin. A familiar fever hit my core, and my vaginal muscles contracted.

"No thong tonight, darling. Will you give me a private tour of the rooms in this building?"

"Of course, my love. Before we leave, do you see this ice sculpture right here?"

"Yes." I glanced at the figure of a naked woman.

"It's the mythical Galatea. According to an ancient Greek tale, Pygmalion of Cyprus crafted this beauty with his hands," Julian explained.

"He must have had such skilled fingers," I giggled, touching Julian's chest.

"Indeed. He also fell in love with her."

"What happened to them?"

"Aphrodite breathed life into Galatea and united the couple in marriage." Julian kissed the sensitive spot behind my ear, lighting up my heat.

"Mrs. Richland, you are my Galatea."

"And you, professor, are my maker." I caressed the lapel of Julian's jacket and adjusted his bowtie.

"I want to fuck you," Julian whispered into my ear. My husband's words sent tingles up my spine.

"I want you, too." I stared into his hauntingly seductive espresso eyes, then kissed his lips.

He returned the kiss with a searing hotness, and his supple tongue probed in my mouth, gently sucking and playing. His thumb circled the base of my neck while we continued our deep French kiss in a passionate clinch.

"Saph …" Julian broke the kiss, scanning the crowded room.

He caressed the curve of my hip in a way only an expert lover knew, sending ripples of ecstasy through me. I glanced at the gold ring on his left hand, which matched the one on mine. Both rings shone with the newness of wedded bliss. We were married at my church a few months before, and Pastor Lewis had done an outstanding job as our wedding celebrant. The ceremony was small and intimate, with family and close friends. Frances wept tears of joy as she'd held Drake, who'd worn a toddler's tuxedo for the occasion. Julian and I would forever remember our wedding day and our honeymoon holiday.

"You look like you're lost in deep thoughts," Julian murmured.

"I was reminiscing about our wonderful summer." I stroked his arm.

"Ah. Did you enjoy Europe?"

"I fell in love with the continent. Rome was fun."

"Let's recreate some of that … fun."

"When in Rome …" I lowered my lashes.

Julian bent his head, and our foreheads touched. His fingers caressed my body, like a sculptor appreciating his work.

"Professor Richland? I need you now. I can't wait anymore." My breathing hitched, and my pussy was wet with want.

"As you wish, Mrs. Richland."

I took Julian's ring-clad hand, and he led the way out of the ballroom. We passed Vera, who raised her eyebrows as we left. I winked, hinting that Julian and I would be up to no good. She grinned, then returned to her conversation with the mayor's wife.

***

"What a lovely room!" I gasped at an ornate office, which was adorned in blue.

"It reminds me of the color of your eyes." Julian smiled, placing his hands in his pockets. All the while, his body touched mine, refusing to break away from any physical contact.

"How did you know about this room?"

"I have my ways."

I walked to a large oak writing desk in the middle of the office and sat on the edge. "You've been here before?" I raised one eyebrow.

"Perhaps."

"Oh, kinky."

"It was another lifetime, Saph. I've taken you here because I want you." His eyes followed mine, refusing to let go.

"Julian ..."

"It's just you. Only you. It was always you."

His eyes glowed with pure, raw lust in the darkness. I tried to move, but he barred me from going anywhere by placing both hands on the desk on each side of me, trapping my body. "You're not going anywhere, love," he drawled. His body angled in closer to mine, and his face lit up with a devious grin.

"Julian," I moaned, as his lips descended on my neck. He lightly grazed my skin with his teeth, delving deeper into his kisses. His nimble fingers undid the clasp around my neck, and the top half of my dress fell to my waist, exposing my naked breasts.

"Oh, God, you're so fucking amazing. Incredible," he groaned, feeling the softness of my supple breasts. "Do you know that I'm a possessive man who is madly in love with my woman?"

"I do, darling." I smiled, stroking my husband's hair.

"I am nothing more than a madman, crazy about my Galatea."

"I know." My fingers played with the nape of his neck, teasing the dark curls of his short hair.

"Touch me, Saph." Julian unzipped his pants and took my right hand to feel his thick arousal. His pleading eyes reminded me of dark chocolate, deliciously enticing with a slight hint of bittersweetness. A glimmer of light from the office window highlighted his sharp cheekbones, accentuating his handsome, tan face.

I wrapped my hand around his hot hardness, while he planted my neck with voracious kisses, casting another enchanting spell on my soul. The tenderness was gone when he slipped my dress down my hips, which fell to my ankles.

"Look what we have here!" Julian removed his jacket and whipped a silk scarf out of the inner pocket. His wide grin was sinful and charming, arousing a twist of erotic pleasure between my thighs.

"Will you tie me up, professor?" I teased, standing naked and unafraid. I straightened my back and shoulders, showing off my full breasts, ripe for the picking.

Julian gazed at my body, groaned with pleasure, and salaciously licked his lips. "Turn around, Sapphire. You have been very bad for being late this evening," he commanded.

I followed Julian's instructions and he roughly tied my hands behind my back.

"Now, bend."

"Yes, Professor Richland." I spread my legs and bent as far as I could forward until one side of my face rested on the oak office desk. I felt his cock tease my buttocks first, rubbing against them before it slid into my slick, wet pussy.

"Fuck, you're so tight and snug." Julian groaned, grabbing my hips with both hands. He began thrusting hard at a steady rate, then picked up the pace, making love to me with rigorous energy.

"Whose cock do you want?" He grunted.

"Yours."

"Hmm?" He thrust harder and deeper into me.

"Ow!" I cried, feeling his penis pushing against my cervix. It was an ounce of pain, followed by a wave of pleasure. The scent of sex and sweat filled the air around us, and I heard his skin slapping against mine.

"Whose cock do you need?" Julian teased with his wicked words and dangerous cock, which drove in and out of me.

"*Yours!* Only yours, Julian!" I yelled in between gasps as his hands tightened their grip on my ass. He spanked my right ass cheek, lightly at first; then, I felt the stinging pain of the second smack.

"My body suffers without you, Sapphire!" Julian cried as he continued pounding into me. "It's because my soul is in your body."

"You have me," I said, breathing heavily with each thrust.

"Always. You are my beloved wife," he whispered, then kissed the sensitive spot behind my ear.

We continued our deep and raw fucking until our bodies both surrendered to the thrill of our climaxes.

As my body recovered from the intensity of our lovemaking, a heightened sensation swelled in my heart. For as long as I could remember, Julian had always shown me a side to himself—things he never showed any other lover—that revealed his strengths, weaknesses, vulnerabilities, and power. For all his sweet seduction, intelligence, ambrosial allure, and flaws, he loved and trusted me so deeply that he revealed his entire soul only to me. Love and sex with Julian was provocative, stimulating, and empowering. I'd married my match.

The following morning

At home, Julian and I rested in our bed. I snuggled on his chest, breathing in his heady scent.

"The look on Vera's face was priceless when we returned to the ballroom last night," I commented.

"She didn't expect us to return." Julian's expression remained cool and unphased.

"She and Alistair make a lovely couple."

"He's a good man. Vera needs someone strong who respects her."

"According to Vera, you were ruthless with her dates before she met Alistair." I held my breath, trying not to giggle.

"Alistair can thank me for it." He released a soft chuckle. I turned my head up and gazed at Julian. "What?" He peered at me.

"For a man who used to be a womanizer, you are very protective," I mock-teased.

"I'm only protective of those I love." He rubbed my arm and kissed my forehead.

I listened to my husband's heartbeat as we lay in peaceful quietness for a minute.

"You asked me once if I believe in God," Julian spoke, breaking our blissful silence. "I believe in God and the devil, the angels and the saints, and heaven and hell. I've been through hell, and I found heaven with you, Saph."

"I'm just a woman, Julian."

"No, darling. You are my angel. You are my miracle."

He lowered his eyes and pressed his lips on mine. There's one thing about Julian Carpenter Richland. He is my Pygmalion. There is no other man like him.

Epilogue

Julian
Five years later

It's been about a decade since I first met my wife.

I once told Saph I couldn't promise marriage, kids, and a house with a white picket fence. She joked the other day, telling me to "eat my words."

God, I love her.

So, what's happened since I married my angel?

We moved to Port Willington, on the west coast, after Alistair suggested a change of scenery. He hinted that Willington State University's archaeology department needed a senior lecturer. Naturally, I took the opportunity. With several published papers under my belt, I've been busy traveling for work conferences and teaching classes.

Saph and I had another boy, Lewis—named after Pastor Peter Lewis. He and Drake are close, but they clash from time to time. It's the usual sibling rivalry, reminding me of Vera and myself when we were kids.

Saph found a job at the university's main library, which makes the commute to and from work more manageable since we're both employed on campus.

She enjoys a peaceful life, which came with the changes.

We did the right thing to leave our past behind in Lester Harbor for a quieter lifestyle in Port Willington.

Sapphire

"See you on Monday, Lydia." I waved at my assistant after finishing my shift.

I then turned to Julian, who'd picked me up at the library on the way home.

He slung my heavy bag on his shoulder. "What's in here, love? It feels like a bag of bricks."

It was filled with wet wipes, gluten-free snacks, Julian's old book, *Quo Vadis*, and my laptop.

"Drake has his first piano lesson tomorrow, so shall I take him, or will you?" Julian asked as we walked to the car park.

"We can go together. I want to see our son play his first note." I smiled, twisting the key on the chain around my neck.

Julian took my hand and stroked my tattooed wrist. He and I now have each other's names permanently inked on the underside of our right wrists.

"Julian, when is Frances coming to visit us?"

"Next month."

"Good. I look forward to having family over." I smiled, remembering Frances, Vera, and Alistair.

My own dysfunctional, fucked-up family may have disowned me, but I came out richer than poorer.

I'm grateful every day for what I have, because we don't know what tomorrow brings.

Vita brevis. Life is short.

The End

www.blackvelvetseductions.com

About the author

Estelle Pettersen is an Australian author and former journalist whose romance stories explore empowerment, freedom, and finding one's strength. She has a Bachelor of Arts degree, majoring in Journalism and Psychology, from the University of Queensland, Australia. Her second degree is an MBA from Queensland University of Technology, Australia. She is a member of Romance Writers of Australia and is passionate about history, languages, cultures, traveling, food, and wine. She is happily married and living in Norway these days.

More Black Velvet Seductions titles

Their Lady Gloriana by Starla Kaye
Cowboys in Charge by Starla Kaye
Her Cowboy's Way by Starla Kaye
Punished by Richard Savage, Nadia Nautalia & Starla Kaye
Accidental Affair by Leslie McKelvey
Right Place, Right Time by Leslie McKelvey
Her Sister's Keeper by Leslie McKelvey
Playing for Keeps by Glenda Horsfall
Playing By His Rules by Glenda Horsfall
The Stir of Echo by Susan Gabriel
Rally Fever by Crea Jones
Behind The Clouds by Jan Selbourne
Trusting Love Again by Starla Kaye
Runaway Heart by Leslie McKelvey
The Otherling by Heather M. Walker
First Submission - Anthology
These Eyes So Green by Deborah Kelsey
Dark Awakening by Karlene Cameron
The Reclaiming of Charlotte Moss by Heather M. Walker
Ryann's Revenge by Rai Karr & Breanna Hayse
The Postman's Daughter by Sally Anne Palmer
Final Kill by Leslie McKelvey
Killer Secrets by Zia Westfield
Crossover, Texas by Freia Hooper-Bradford
The Caretaker by Carol Schoenig
The King's Blade by L.J. Dare
Uniform Desire - Anthology
Safe by Keren Hughes
Finishing the Game by M.K. Smith
Out of the Shadows by Gabriella Hewitt
A Woman's Secret by C.L. Koch
Her Lover's Face by Patricia Elliott
Naval Maneuvers by Dee S. Knight

www.blackvelvetseductions.com

Perilous Love by Jan Selbourne
Patrick by Callie Carmen
The Brute and I by Suzanne Smith
Home by Keren Hughes
Only A Good Man Will Do by Dee S. Knight
Secret Santa by Keren Hughes
Killer Lies by Zia Westfield
A Merman's Choice by Alice Renaud
All She Ever Needed by Lora Logan
Nicolas by Callie Carmen
Paging Dr. Turov by Gibby Campbell
Out of the Ashes by Keren Hughes
A Thread of Sand by Alan Souter
Stolen Beauty by Piper St. James
Mystic Desire anthology
Killer Deceptions by Zia Westfield
Edgeplay by Annabel Allan
Music for a Merman by Alice Renaud
Joseph by Callie Carmen
Not You Again! by Patricia Elliott
The Unveiling of Amber by Viola Russell
Husband Material by Keren Hughes
Never Have I Ever by Julia McBryant
Hard Limits by Annabel Allan
Anthony by Callie Carmen
Paper Hearts by Keren Hughes
The King's Spy by L.J. Dare
More Than Words by Keren Hughes & Jodie Harrold

Our back catalog is being released on Kindle Unlimited
You can find us on:
Twitter: BVSBooks
Facebook: Black Velvet Seductions
See our bookshelf on Amazon now!
Search "BVS Black Velvet Seductions Publishing Company"

www.blackvelvetseductions.com

www.ingramcontent.com/pod-product-compliance
Lightning Source LLC
Chambersburg PA
CBHW022108170626
46808CB00002B/648